LOVE I

Margot bent slightly to peer into the window. Pete faced her, his arms locked around a girl, as they swayed – naked – to soft tunes that Margot tried to recognize but couldn't. She felt herself growing excited as she watched him slide his hand down the girl's back to her buttocks and splay open the dimpled cheeks.

The girl leaned back, tilting her head.

'Oh, my God,' Margot whispered, suddenly short of breath. Shock flew through her as she stared at the naked couple. For there, in Pete's embrace, was Sally . . .

Love in
the Saddle

Anonymous

HEADLINE

Copyright © 1990 Red Stripe Books

First published in 1991
by HEADLINE BOOK PUBLISHING PLC

Published by arrangement with
CAROL PUBLISHING GROUP, INC, NY, NY, USA

10 9 8 7 6 5 4 3 2 1

ISBN 0 7472 3700 X

Printed and bound in Great Britain by
Collins Manufacturing, Glasgow

HEADLINE BOOK PUBLISHING PLC
Headline House
79 Great Titchfield Street
London W1P 7FN

Love in
the Saddle

CHAPTER 1

Swiftly, Margot gathered her black waist-length hair at the nape of her neck and tied a navy ribbon around it. Then, glancing at the clock by her double bed, she reached for her gray suede chaps she had carelessly thrown in the corner when she came back with Corey last night, and zipped them to their snug fit around each of her blue-jeaned legs.

"Corey, get up," she ordered, staring intensely at the tall figure wrapped in the sheets in her bed. "Get up. This is my bed, and my horse farm, and you're my employee. Now, for the tenth time, get up, get to the stables, start cleaning the stalls and exercising the horses."

"Margot, don't be so rough on me," he murmured, brushing his wavy blond hair off his forehead, as his face appeared from beneath the sheets. He smiled wanly.

Margot brushed her hand across her pale face with its long, sharp nose and perfect white teeth. "Come on. It's already 5:30. I need to start the day now because I've got fourteen horses to ride today. You've got a lot of work to do to keep up with me." She bent over him. "Just because I screw you does not mean you can shirk your job. I'm still your boss."

Yes, she thought, I'm his boss. Corey's, Craig's and Pete's boss, and Sally's. My grooms. Not bad for a thirty-year-old: four grooms, fifty horses to ride and train, three top riding students, and a two hundred-

1

acre horse farm with lush pastures, green paddocks, glistening stables and an enormous indoor riding arena. No, not bad at all.

Now, though, she had no time to applaud herself. For she had too much to do today, as every day. She bent down and wisked off the covers from long, lean Corey. A swift, almost automatic surge of desire coursed through her. Yup, it was true that she had to get out and start her day, but it was also true that every time she looked at Corey—whether he was cleaning bridles in the tack room or mucking out stalls with a rake—she heated up. She smiled to herself, acknowledging the fact that she'd probably known all along: no point in going through the day hot.

Swiftly, she bent over and pressed her lips to his sleeping shaft, tickling the end with her teasing tongue til it bulged with anticipation.

"Thought we had to get to the stables," he murmured, his fingers moving to Margot's luxurious hair. They began to massage her head as her lips soundlessly flew over his rod.

She dropped to the side of the bed, on her knees. "All right, I guess we do have some time," she whispered, as Corey reached out and pulled her T-shirt out of her pants.

He slipped his fingers upward til he dipped them between the lacy covering in which her breasts nestled. He found their tips, peaking with anticipation, and fondled them as she hurriedly pulled down her jeans, never releasing him from her mouth. Their breath came in short gasps, waiting for the explosion that they knew was barely moments away.

Margot inched away, watching his rod throb upward, waiting. She clambered on him, sitting astride. He reached for her breasts, fondling them with impassioned fingers. Quickly, she took him and guided him inside her and then jammed down hard with deep thrusts til the waves of heat overcame them. With satisfaction, she felt him clutch her and listened to him groan. She had the touch all right. But so did he.

Grinning, she wiped beads of perspiration from her brow and wiggled off onto the sheets beside him.

She smiled. "You're just one of the benefits of having my own grooms." Yes, she smiled smugly, pulling her clothes on again. She could fuck them whenever she wanted. All of them, except Sally. Sally wouldn't have her. And right now, Sally was the only one she really wanted.

"Wanna do it again?" He smiled tentatively, as if he hoped that he might talk her into a marathon day of sex in her comfortable four-poster double bed instead of mucking out stalls. But without waiting for an answer, he shrugged and reluctantly spoke. "Guess I wasn't good enough, was I? Not good enough to keep you here for another round? I'll meet you in the barn in ten minutes."

She smiled in return, then bent to place a swift kiss on his nose. "Thanks for breakfast, Corey."

Margot sauntered into her spacious barn, noting with satisfaction that Craig and Pete had already mucked out the stalls in their areas, and were now distributing grain and vitamins. She scanned the aisle for Sally. Ah, Sally.

Even as she thought of her, she found her heart

3

lurch at the prospect of seeing her: bouncy, perky, wild red-haired, and freckled. She swallowed, trying to quell that diffuse sense of longing that seemed to invade her whenever she thought of Sally.

She shrugged absently. Oh well, you always want what you can't get. Still, glancing now, Margot saw that her fingers had clenched into fists, an effort of will until the physical longing disappeared.

"Sally here?" she called out brusquely to no one in particular.

"Yup," Craig called out from High Flyer's stall "In Mighty Mike's."

Margot saw a couple cans of grain drop into the horse's feed bin, then heard the hose as Craig filled up the bucket. She peeked in. "Where's a salt block?"

"I'm just gonna get one. He dropped his out of the rack and then stomped on it," Craig grinned. "Like he always does."

Margot eyed Craig's stocky body, so compact and muscular that she sometimes wondered how he could mount a horse and ride as gracefully as he did. His blue jean work shirt was unbuttoned to the waist. Perspiration already dotted his bare chest, though the summer morning had scarcely started.

"Gonna be hot today, Margot," he noted. "Where's Corey?"

She shrugged, as if she didn't know. But does Craig? she wondered. How many times could she fuck Corey without Craig and Pete not knowing? Did each of them think he was the only one? How would they react to find out that she balled the others?

Insulted or amused? Relieved, maybe? She snorted,

as she walked down the aisle, looking into each horse's stall as she did every morning. For how in the world could each of them have the audacity to think he, alone, was good enough, clever enough and resilient enough for her?

"Please get Midnight ready," was her only response to the observation of the summer day. After all, business was business, and she didn't chitchat when she had fourteen horses to ride and three students to teach. "I want to ride him first."

"He's ready. Sally's warmed him up."

"Sally! Why Sally? Midnight is in your barn section."

"Well," Craig came to the stall door, as the horse lunged for the grain bin, "she finished her stalls already and I hadn't. I didn't think you cared who groomed and tacked him, or who lunged him."

Margot pursed her lips. It was true, she didn't. But why should Sally have the privilege of readying a horse for her when she wouldn't do—the other stuff. She turned on her heel for the ring.

She stopped at the door and watched Sally. Sally Winthrop had been here ten months. She had finished high school early and set out to learn how to train horses. Margot had never seen anyone work harder or learn faster or have more natural talent. Sure, they started out that way—gung-ho and willing. And then, three months into it, they began to lag. If it got too bad, Margot fired them. She never let her horses get in the way of her other after-hours activities.

But not Sally. She still busted her butt. And the funny thing was that she never let anything get in the

5

way of the horses either — at least she didn't let Margot.

Margot leaned against the sliding door, watching Sally manipulate the lines with the draw reins to position Midnight's head properly. The guys always rushed to get on Midnight, but Sally knew that the ground work was key. She never rode him, just worked him on the ground. Still Margot resented it. She wanted to be the one to tell Sally how to work Midnight; it wasn't Sally's choice.

"That's enough, Sally. I'll get on now. Thanks." Margot strode into the center of the ring, unfastening the lunging apparatus so she could ride.

"What do you think, Margot? After a rough start, he really had his nose tucked in. Really looked collected." Sally laughed. She always laughed when she was pleased. A tinkling, merry laugh that Margot yearned to cup in her hands and save. An infectious laugh that made everyone happy and made Margot resentful and jealous.

"It's OK," she replied curtly, swinging her suede-clad leg over the horse's back. She slipped her feet into stirrips.

"Should I set up any jumps?" Sally headed for a cross rail in the far corner.

"No." Careful, Margot she warned herself. If you're too nasty, she'll leave. Be pleasant. "No, thanks, Sally. You did a good job on him. I think we'll do some ground work. I want to begin some dressage training now. What do you think?" She forced herself to say.

But what she really wanted to say was that for ten months she had hungered for that pert little body with that pert little ass and perky breasts and rosebud mouth. For ten months Sally had sidestepped her, seemingly oblivious to Margot's subtle offers. She'd decline Margot's offer to join her in a midnight swim in the lake; turn down her offer to join her in the trailer at the last horse show rather than sleep next to the horses' stalls with Craig to protect them if necessary; refuse a shopping trip in town and a drink after work.

Margot ground her cheek bones into the saddle, as much to bring the horse's legs beneath him as to wipe out her own heat at her core.

She gently pressed her calves into the flanks of Midnight, sending him on a leisurely walk. She pulled herself up straight, throwing her shoulders back, arching her back slightly, balancing herself in the center of the horse.

She pressed her calves again, slightly stronger, sending the horse into a trot. Margot posted, rising and falling back into the saddle with each step. She pulled her whip out of her blue jean pocket and gently flicked him on his rear, once again asking him to put his legs beneath his backside, driving him forward into the bridle so that he tucked his nose in, accepting the bit.

She saw Sally watching, her mouth open in admiration as she worked the horse, and began to work on side passing, crossing one front leg over the other. Slowly, steadily, patiently, just a bit each day, ending on a high note. Finally, with a flourish, she stopped Midnight in the center of the ring.

"Sally, will you ask Craig to get Sweet Revenge ready, and set up some three- and four-foot jumps

7

for me, please?" Margot threw her right leg over the saddle and slipped to the ground effortlessly. She patted Midnight's neck.

"Sure, Margot. What time is Steven coming for his lesson?"

"About 7:30. I think I have time to ride one more horse. Will you lunge High Flyer before Steven gets here?"

Steven, her star pupil. He was eighteen, no younger than Sally, but with a difference. He was off-limits. Irrevocably off-limits. She couldn't afford to botch her future or his because of a romp in the hay. This was Steven's last year to compete for the Medal and McClay awards, the last year he could catapult Margot into impossibly high realms of success as not only a horse trainer, but as a trainer of students as well.

She hadn't always been so decisive about the division between students and teacher. She grimaced now when she thought of William six years ago. Where was William now? Then, he'd been Walt's student, and Margot was apprenticed to Walt as assistant trainer. William was headed for the highest reaches of success—trying to make the Olympics Team.

Margot would watch their lessons with great concentration. She concentrated equally on William's taut thighs and chest, wiry frame and short black hair that fit snugly under his black hunt cap. She felt those hot flashes when she accidently touched him in the tack room or when they were wrapping polos around his horse's front legs so he wouldn't kick himself when he jumped.

8

William was in the tack room one day, cleaning his saddle which was propped on a rack in front of him. Margot walked in, for they were alone; everyone had departed for the lunch hour. She hungered for him. She'd been hungry for a few months, ever since she'd broken up with her boyfriend of years and years. That pressure was always there, that need to press her thighs together tightly so that she could focus on her job.

"Hi, William," she smiled, her deep voice breaking the stillness.

"Margot," he nodded, wiping his cloth on saddle soap.

"Need help? I can do the flap, if you like." She'd made up her mind. She would have him.

She walked to his side, lifting the flap upwards so that it brushed against the front of his breeches. He jerked backward, surprised.

"Sorry," she dropped the flap and reached out, patting his pants, as if to sooth a pain. But she didn't drop her hand.

William, still young and so innocent, just stared. And hardened beneath her hand. She gazed at his short black hair, his straight nose and dark brown eyes, saw his face flush in recognition of what was happening to him.

"Did I hurt you?" she breathed, stretching upward so that her breath glanced off his ear.

He shook his head, unmoving. The cloth in his hand lay untouched on top of the saddle. The wholesome, slightly acrid smell of leather cleaners wafted about them.

Margot turned slightly and deftly unzipped his fly

9

even as she fondled the stiffening rod within his pants. His member bulged helplessly inside its tight constraints. Then, slowly, Margot reached inside his breeches and removed it. She stared in delight at its length, throbbing with purple veins. She gripped it in her hands, pulling slightly, toying with the end, as she wiggled out of her own jeans and panties and threw them to the floor of the tack room.

She jumped up on the saddle, facing backward so that she rested against the pommel, and signaled him to join her. He hesitated, still aghast at the future just moments away from him. But a second later, his long leg swung over the saddle, and the damp cloth he'd held, smeared with saddle soap, lay on the floor.

They faced each other on the leather saddle perched on the saddle rack beneath them. Margot slipped her hand into the waist of his breeches and ran her strong fingers around his flat belly til she heard his quick intake of breath, and saw him jut forward, looking for a place to jam his rod, now prancing about wildly.

Margot felt hot, passionately hot. She relished the tack room with its pristine gray painted tack trunks, the bits and reins and saddles hanging from hooks, the saddle pads lying on tables. Her own wetness seeped from her cavity as she placed her arms around his shoulders, pulling herself toward him to plant feverish kisses on his lips.

Suddenly, kisses weren't enough. She, too, needed to put their bodies together. She looked down as she gripped his cock, edging it toward her mound. She could wait no longer. She arched forward, slipping his cock inside her moist hole. She pressed down til he filled her up and she shuddered with the delight of feeling that hard rod within her. She pressed against him, wriggling til he was in her up to the hilt. She took a hand and placed it under her bra and waited as he began to fiddle with the tips of her breasts til they stood in taut points.

She placed her finger into his belly button, heard him groan, and then, methodically, they began to ram against each other, harder and more furiously until the overwhelming fires splashed through them.

They didn't do it again, ever. Walt had seen. He'd ambled back to the barn and watched her seduce William. Then he told William he'd drop him as a student of horses if they ever did it again, that he needed all his concentration for horses, not sex. Then Walt turned to Margot and told her that now it was his turn.

He dismissed William, closed the door to the tack room and pulled out his soft member, an evil smile pasted on his smooth face. His bald head, edged with just a fringe of brown hair, seemed to glow with ugly excitement.

Obediently, wordlessly, terrified that he would fire her for disobeying him, Margot fell to her knees on the sawdust and took him in her mouth. His rod was as long and spindley as he was. She ran her tongue over the shaft, her fingers on his scrotom til he hardened and came in her mouth with sickening lust. She thought she'd retch, but she said nothing. It was part of her job. And she had determined she would do anything, absolutely anything, to get ahead in this business. After all, it was just a blow job. She could put it out of her thoughts.

11

Margot stayed with Walt another year, for she needed to learn more about horse training. An uneasy alliance of blow jobs and hand jobs in the darkness of a horse's stall, while she listened to the sounds of hay being munched and water slurped, or else in the bright lights of the tack room while Walt polished a bridle. She's suck him or rub him til he came. That was all. Nothing for her. But she saw the advantage of being the boss.

She saw herself named assistant trainer well before the other girls. She saw that she was given permission to train horses that Walt had always coveted for himself. She shrugged. What she did with her mouth and her hands was just as important as what she did when she worked a horse. It all got her ahead faster.

William and she scarcely ever talked again. They both feared for their careers. And they knew Walt was right. William didn't have time to think about girls at the barn. He needed to think about riding. Shortly afterward, he received the awards he'd hoped for and then went off to law school and probably never rode again. But Margot learned from that. She wouldn't risk anything with her students. Trainers, yes; grooms, yes; customers, even. Not students.

Now, Margot stretched comfortably after the long day. The shower had been the relief she needed. She saw the water peel off the layers of raw dust and sweat that accumulated when she rode on brutally hot days under the sun relentlessly pressing down. She glanced down at her watch, slightly blurred from the splashes of water.

She was meeting Rob for dinner to discuss ways to increase the prize moneys at some of the regional

12

horse shows. She liked Rob. He owned Acres Wild, about ten miles down the road. He'd tried to buy her out a couple years ago, but he couldn't persuade her to sell. All the money he offered wasn't enough to staunch the dream she'd always nurtured of having her own farm. After a willful battle, they'd settled into a comfortable relationship of friendly competitors.

Swiftly, she pulled on a loose jean dress, letting her breasts hang freely beneath the material. She combed her hair into a high ponytail, slipped on some sandals and made her way to the front porch to wait for Rob. She eased into a rocking chair, as she sipped a glass of lemonade. She'd wait for Rob, but she'd think about Herbert. For it was Herbert who laughingly had given her a rocking chair as a house present.

Thrilled, for she'd never had a rocking chair, she'd sat down hard sending the chair flying across the porch, leaving her on the wide boards on the floor, her feet upended, her elbows propping her up.

"Is this a trick chair?" she murmured, smiling a puzzled smile. She stood, walked over, gingerly placed her hands on the frame to still its movement and sat down. She waited for it to explode. But it didn't. But neither did it move as it was supposed to. Quizzically, she glanced up at Herbert, standing amused, arms akimbo, watching the scene with delicious fascination.

"What happens now?" She asked. She felt rather like a five-year-old than the twenty five-year-old she was then. Now what? Her feet were firmly planted on the ground and she had no idea how to rock the chair.

Herbert leaned against the porch fence, head thrown back in gales of laughter. "Can't believe it," he drawled in his Southern accent, running his fingers through his thick white hair. "I just gave a rockin' chair to the one person in 'Merica who has no idea how to rock." He laughed again. "Ever'one knows how to rock!" He grabbed the sides of his heavyset body as he guffawed some more.

Margot laughed too, her eyes resting fondly on the older man. Her financier, her supporter, the man who'd made the dreams of this farm come true. He'd seen her ride at Walt's, bought some of her horses, and thought she'd make a fine trainer in her own right. He bought her all of this. And it hardly cost Margot anything.

Now, she rocked gently back and forth, having mastered the art of moving the chair slowly. Rocking had been harder to learn than riding, she giggled again, remembering the nights she had sneaked out here when Herbert was sleeping so she could practice. Then one day she got it. They both celebrated on the rocker, screwing at fast speeds, slow speeds and abrupt changes of speed.

"Hey, Margot!" Ron called from the cab on his jeep. "Ready?"

"Yup!" She jumped up, grabbed her straw purse and climbed in the front seat. "Smells like a skunk in here," she smiled, her white teeth flashing.

"Good nose. Skunk sprayed the dog. The only way I could get the dog home was in the car. Sorry," he grinned sheepishly, his straight brown hair brushed back off his face, his aqualine nose looking even longer, his Adam's apple bobbing as it always did when he spoke.

Margot leaned over and pecked him on the cheek. "Let's go to your place, then we'll talk," she smiled demurely. "I need a little hors d'oeuvre."

CHAPTER 2

That same music wafted familiarly from the corner juke box. The pinball machine clicked with an unsteady rhythm. The television above the bar glowed gently and soundlessly. Low, rhythmic voices of familiar people at the bar and the surrounding tables filled the air.

Margot stretched out her legs beneath the heavily shellacked wooden table and leaned against the straight-backed banquette, toying with spaghetti strands mired in gooey tomato sauce. She smiled to herself. The food wasn't too good here, but it made her feel safe and cared for in its dreary familiarity.

She kicked off her brown sandal, toying with it with her toes, as she shifted in her seat. Herbert droned on about a new real estate investment in Florida. He could be interesting at times, but tonight was not one of them.

She nodded her head with feigned interest. Still, he was a good sport when they had sex, and she did have a large obligation to him for the farm.

"Not too hungry, Margot?" Herbert stopped mid-sentence and ran his hand through his thick white hair. He wasn't young anymore, but the lines on his face gave him a rugged cragginess that Margot liked. He was still a hulk unclothed with a massive, bull-like chest, thin hips and good humor.

"Not for this, anyway," she smiled and winked. "I'd love some coffee at your house, if that's OK," she added, already picturing the soft beauty of his house — with an entire wall of windows — perched just to the side of the waterfall of the Raleigh Stream.

"Let me get the check, then." Herbert motioned to the waitress. "Lallie, check here, please."

Suddenly, Margot's movements were arrested. The toes that toyed with her sandal halted midair. For she heard that tinkling laugh. Her heart stopped, as if an electric current had jolted it. For without turning, she knew instantly that it was Sally's tinkling, merry little laugh. And she was with someone else.

She swallowed, hoping that Herbert would be too busy fishing for dollars and change to notice her attention elsewhere. Sally's laugh — saved for everyone but herself. Margot had to see her, to be noticed by her.

With effort, she turned her head and saw Sally's perky little rear end bobbing as she slid into a seat with — Margot craned her neck, but the banquette seat was in the way. Who? She strained forward, trying to hear if it were a male or female voice. Then, that laugh again. And that stab of pain through her body as if the laugh wielded a knife. What was it about Sally that enticed her so? Why did Sally reject her so bluntly?

Margot squirmed, pressing her legs together at the thought of Sally as sudden moisture gathered

16

between them. Abruptly, she stood. "Ready?" She had to get out of here. The familiarity which, minutes ago, had been so comforting, now seemed alien and cold.

As they edged out the door, through the crowd of local horse people and merchants gathered at the bar or waiting for tables, she glanced toward Sally and saw an unknown girl with her.

How could this happen? she raged at herself. How could Sally be with another woman? And how could I have let myself become so enamoured of her, so hot for her? Never before had she known such frustration.

She ought to fire Sally so she wouldn't face that daily torment of desperately wanting her and being teased by her. But she couldn't. She didn't think she could bear not seeing her every day—even this way.

Margot stopped at the table. "Why, hello, Sally." Margot tried to keep her voice even, when, really, she longed to smack her face, then grab her and kiss her hard on the mouth, as her fingers kneaded her well-formed breasts.

"Hi, Margot," Sally smiled a dazzling smile. "Do you know Eva? She works at Rob's."

Margot turned toward the lanky girl with the straight, mouselike hair and pale, sickly complexion. Not much competition, at least. "How do you do?" She turned back toward Sally and smiled her widest, grandest smile. "I hope you two have a nice night. See you in the morning, then."

That girl, she worked for Rob. Then Margot could find out more about her, see where she fit into Sally's life. She turned and waved. Sally was all-consuming.

17

Barely an hour went by that she didn't think of that girl in some fashion. Some remark, some quirky body movement, that lovely little laugh.

Now Margot bit her lip and turned toward Herbert. Goddamn it, how long would Sally taunt her? She slid into the white Jaguar next to him. "I'm ready for a big one, tonight," she whispered.

"Me too." As Herbert reached for the ignition, Margot reached for the fly of his pants and extricated his prick. He smiled good-humoredly. Nimbly, she bent over and licked it til she felt it thicken.

"Margot, not here," Herbert stammered hoarsely, as he attempted to back out of the parking space.

"Why not?" Margot grinned. "This is where I want to start. Right now." A fierce desire overtook her. It wasn't passion or unbearable heat. It was vengeance, a way to wipe out the spectre of Sally. She wanted to fuck herself into oblivion. She drove her mouth over his shaft, fully inserting him and felt him pulsate as she mouthed him.

"Oh, Margot," he breathed, one hand on her luxuriant black hair, the other on the wheel. "Can't you wait ten minutes?" He gripped her hair, trying to pull her off him. But she wouldn't relinquish, gripping him firmly between her lips. The car jolted forward, then slowed, as he regained some control.

"Margot!" Herbert repeated huskily. The car lurched forward erratically as Margot's tongue caressed his cock languidly, then furiously. His hand on her head tried to pull her off again as the car swerved. Suddenly, he stopped the car on the side of the road, acknowledging her power. He pressed her head to him as she took his entire shaft in her mouth. Fiercely, Margot sucked him til her own anger was vented. She felt him lurch forward, felt his thigh muscles tighten, heard him grunt his release. She withdrew from him.

"Margot," Herbert pouted, eyeing his still swollen member. "That's dangerous."

"Why? Do you have a disease I might catch?" She asked innocently, patting his shoulder. "Now put it away before we get arrested."

She heaved a sigh. She felt better, for the moment. The anger was gone. Now, what remained was the dull ache of heat, unspent passion that she intended to use.

She stared out of the window next to her. The sky was still streaked with purple and gold, remnants of another spicy hot summer day. Yeah, she felt better. But it wasn't good enough. She leaned across her bucket seat and kissed him on the cheek. She laid her cheek against his. "I want you," she whispered. "I want to do it til we can't move anymore."

"Hey, Margot, I'm no spring chicken." Herbert patted her knee.

"I'll make you into one," she retorted, slipping her fingers between the buttons of his red plaid shirt. And she knew she could. Herbert, for one, could do it almost any time.

Margot peered out of the massive picture window in Herbert's bedroom to the waterfall that dropped three stories to the first floor of his redwood home. It was palatially large, with overstuffed couches and chairs, enormous fireplaces and beds. And always, you could hear the splashes and gurgles of the water cascading around you. She headed for the bed, covered in a deep navy quilt with red pillows.

"I need a fuck, Herbert. Can you do it?"

"Try me," he retorted, slipping out of his clothes instantly.

"Herbert, I've been around and I don't think I've met anyone who can fuck as much as you can," Margot grinned in delight, as she sat cross-legged on his bed.

Herbert crossed the floor, naked, his rod already at attention. His barrel chest, with the heavy coat of white hair, heaved with excitement. He stood in front of her, bent over and kissed her moist lips, slipping the straps of her red and white checked dress off her shoulders, down to her waist. Her firm breasts pointed upward.

Margot's breath caught in her throat, as she waited for him to reach down and take her nipples between his fingers and knead them til they crested in firm peaks. She strained, her mouth seeking his. As his tongue slipped in between her lips, finding her tongue, she firmly pressed her mouth against his.

Margot heard her breath quicken, felt that wonderful, well-known tingling in her quim, and arched down against the bed. But Herbert didn't stop toying with her breasts. Now she wanted his fingers to run up her thighs, to find her snatch and her ass. Margot rolled her hips, seeking friction to release her.

But still Herbert toyed with her breasts, til Margot rolled back and forth as the heat invaded her thighs and legs, and arms and stomach. She groaned for more and reached for Herbert's cock, but he neatly sidestepped her. Moaning, she slipped the heel of her foot against her cunt and pressed it hard, waiting for Herbert to shift positions and shove himself inside. But he didn't. And then, the lust overtook her and the huge heat suffused her body. She rolled backward, even as Herbert still kneaded her nipples and fondled her breasts and kissed her lips. She arched madly, her legs bent beneath her in a crab walk, til, at last, she came with a giant groan of splendid contentment.

Finally she eyed him, his prick still rigid. "Now," she whispered, "let's fuck." She pulled his arms, throwing him down on the bed and slid on top of him, inserting his prick as she did. She gripped his shoulders with ferocity as the unwelcome image of Sally skirted across her vision. Then, wordlessly, she pumped against Herbert hard, fierce, meanly til he came and she came.

"OK," he said, "I've had enough for the night." He lay on his back, his head and folded arms, staring toward the waterfall sliding over glistening rocks.

"Oh, Herbert, not really," Margot said, lifting her hair behind her. "I thought you could do more." She burned for more. The hatred and envy she felt for Sally became Margot's hot need.

"I can, but I've done it twice in about an hour. Not bad for a guy my age," he grinned.

She grinned back, a core of dissatisfaction brewing. She hadn't had enough yet. Tonight, coming once or twice wasn't enough. She needed to pound it out, pound out Sally. "Once more, snoockers," she laughingly pouted, her fingers drifting to Herbert's thigh. She ran them lightly over his thighs.

"Gad, Margot, haven't you had enough?" He asked crossly.

"Never with you, Herbert. I think you're great. Let's go for a swim, at least." Margot bounded up, as full of nervous, vicious energy as she had ever been. "Come on," she spoke gently, between clenched teeth. She wanted to hammer him hard.

"How about just a shower?"

"A shower under the waterfall?" For she and Herbert had discovered a flat stone where they could comfortably stand on the edge of the falls, letting the water spray around them. Often she wondered what the waters would be like with Rob or Corey or one of the Mason brothers, but she knew that this water and this setting were reserved for Herbert when he was in town in summer, when he wasn't yachting or snorkling or traveling somewhere else. She rarely saw him in winter. That was why, when he was around in the summer, she owed him a lot.

"Herbert, catch me if you can!" Margot sang out merrily, opening the door to the terrace and racing down the steps that led directly to a pool of water at the base of the falls. "Herbert!"

"Ah, Margot, I'm tired."

"I'm not." Her voice had an edge of irritation. She needed to fuck him. The enjoyment would be gone now, as it had been ever since she'd seen Sally. But the frustration—ever mounting—remained.

She heard his heavy thud on the steps as he made his way down, naked in the late evening. Margot caught her breath. He was handsome: bull-like, intractable, strong. "Come join me," she held out her hand for him, felt his strong grip, saw the pectorals

22

in his chest tighten.

Herbert stepped into the pool and together they walked to their smooth rock, pounded by years of cascading Raleigh Stream waters.

"Fuck me, Herbert," Margot stood on tiptoes and breathed in his ear.

"I can't," he shrugged and motioned toward his flaccid member.

"I bet you can," Margot whispering, leaning down til she held his large scrotom in her hands. Her other hand slipped around to his anus, dipping in and out, til she felt his first surge of interest. She moved her hands to his rod, rubbing it til it hardened.

"See, Herbert?" she tittered. "Whenever my students say they can't, I show them they can do something."

"Margot," Herbert said crossly.

"Herbert," she replied. "I need it some more." Margot placed her hand on her own breasts and gently massaged them in front of him. She watched him closely as his eyes widened and he took an involuntary step closer. She stepped back on their rock, still rubbing her breasts upward and sideways, her breathing steady but heavy. She listened for his and saw that Herbert too was breathing harder.

"OK," he said grudgingly.

"Don't do me any favors," she replied haughtily, sidestepping him as he reached forward. She dropped her hand to her mound and touched it, arching her hips forward, closer to him.

"I won't," he answered hoarsely. "I swear it's not just for you."

Margot glanced down and saw his erect and

throbbing prick, water splashing off its sides to the rock below.

"It's OK," she taunted, her own body threatening to burst from her fingers. Inwardly, she cried for release as her fingers played with her breasts and her quim.

"Margot, don't," he whispered urgently, reaching out for the hand between her legs. He kissed each of the fingers. "Come to me."

Margot looked up, a smile creasing her face. "I hoped you'd see it my way," she beamed, hoisting herself up til her legs clasped Herbert around his hips. Then, with the greatest urgency she had known, she pounded deeply against his shaft, over and over, til the frustration and anguish of the night was at last beaten.

CHAPTER 3

"Set the jumps at five strides, with a triple combination in the middle," Margot called out to Sally and Corey from her perch on top of High Flyer's back as she slowly, easily cantered him around the ring.

She pressed her chaps-clad legs around the horse's flanks, loosely rested her fingers on the reins as he rounded the far corner.

"Whoa," she said softly, barely flicking the reins with her pinkies. The horse slowed to a trot, then a walk. Margot turned him toward the center of the ring and, pressing her legs against his sides, asked him to trot. She began the measured rising and sitting movements to his steps. Then, pressing her right leg against his right side, she asked him to side pass, crossing his front feet in front of each other, until they had crossed the ring diagonally.

"Good boy, just great," she cooed, patting his shoulder with a firm hand. "You really have it down."

"Margot, he looks good," Sally volunteered from the far corner as she hoisted a long white pole onto the standard cups which would hold it in place.

"Thanks," Margot said automatically, paying no attention to the compliments. Compliments, infectious smiles, perky butts were not factors in the ring. Later maybe, but not now. Only horses and the high performance of her employees. "Ready?" she called out impatiently as Corey set the last jump in place.

Margot began to trot, turning High Flyer in a large circle and asking him to canter. The slow, steady canter began as they headed over the five-jump course. Each jump was set just the proper distance from the others so that the jump appeared to be just one more stride in the canter. Nothing special, just another canter stride, four feet in the air.

An unfamiliar face appeared in the doorway. Not entirely unfamiliar, only vaguely familiar. She'd seen him before, somewhere. A student's father? Another trainer? A former buyer? The face plagued her as she rode, but only when she finished did Margot stop, handing High Flyer to Sally to walk out until he cooled down.

"Hello?" she held out her hand toward the unfamiliar man. Who was this exceedingly tall, exquisitely built man?

"Margot? I'm Ed Mason—"

"Of course!" she exclaimed. So that's who! The newscaster. Of course he was vaguely familiar. She saw him on every large newsbreaking story on television. God, what was he doing here?

"Herbert suggested I call."

Of course. Herbert, with a finger in every pot. Everyone who was anyone or might possibly be anyone at some future time was Herbert's friend. Herbert, who sent out two thousand Christmas cards a year. Herbert sent him.

"I have a couple new jumpers I want to have shown. He said you were the best around for training and showing. I checked, and he's right. If you're not the absolute best trainer and rider, you're damn close."

Sweat broke out on Margot's palms. Not the sweat of the hot and sultry day that was surrounding her, but the sweat of flattery and nervousness. Ed Mason could buy anything, and he chose her! She knew she had a reputation, but it was always lovely to have it confirmed. It wasn't enough that Herbert sent her clients—for Herbert had invested in her—but that the clients verified Herbert's direction. She swallowed nervously. He was so tall and so famous and so handsome.

Surreptitiously she eyed the tall man whose brown wavy hair was neatly parted, whose lean, hollowed cheeks and lanky build enticed her. Surprised, she felt herself moisten as their arms brushed against each other, skin to skin, on the hot summer day.

"Let me show you around," Margot said

succinctly, guiding him through the stalls, the feed and tack rooms, and finally the office, to discuss financial arrangements.

As the hour drifted to a close, Margot glanced at her watch nervously. She had horses to ride still. But this was business. This was the establishment of a long-term contact. She'd ride late into the night. She'd ask Sally to stay and help her. It was Sally's night for barn check anyway, so she'd have to be around the farm. Sally would help her groom and set up. So when Ed asked her to join him for lunch, she nodded her assent. "But I think I should change first."

Her hair hung hot and heavy on the nape of her neck. Her T-shirt clung to her breasts. Her jeans felt as if they were chafing her.

"No, you look great. We're meeting Herbert at that deli. I'm sure you don't need to dress for that." Ed stood, unwinding his tall, angular body.

Margot closed her eyes quickly, as if to blot out the intense surge of heat suddenly invading her body. Her heart hammered as she saw that taut outline of his thigh in his tight jeans. This is unseemly, she told herself fiercely, pressing her legs together, hoping he wouldn't see. He was horribly attractive, a fact he clearly knew.

Lunch was lighthearted, then he dropped her back at the barn with a wave, assuring her that his horse would arrive next week. Where she should have been elated by the prestige of one of his horses and the additional money, she felt only drained by an undercurrent of frustration.

Now, lunch over, Margot returned to the barn. It

was quiet. The grooms must be out for lunch still. But Pennies from Heaven was tacked up and waiting. Her people knew her plans. They never left her. They'd be back to ready the next horse for riding. Wiping her hands, she headed for the bathroom, just to wipe off her suddenly sweat-covered face. The shower was on.

As she opened the door, she saw Sally behind the opaque curtain. Not everything, of course, but the outline of her perfect breasts, her rounded tempting buttocks, her slim thighs. Margot's breath caught as she saw Sally stand under the pelting water, head thrown back, casually soaping her upper arms, and singing softly.

Finally! An excuse. As if she hadn't seen that the shower was occupied. Margot peeled off her clothes and stepped toward the stall. She'd tell Sally she'd intended to shower, but she was surprised to see her, but that there was no hurry, they could both stand under the cooling water.

Suddenly, Sally noticed her. She clapped her hand over her mouth in surprise. Happy or not? Margot wondered.

Margot drew back the curtain. "Hi." She tried to keep her eyes level with Sally's, tried not to divulge that she itched to suckle at Sally's breasts and lick her quim. She tried to keep her voice from quavering.

Sally stepped back, covering her breasts with her hands. "Oh, gee, I took a few minutes to have a shower. I didn't think you'd mind."

"Of course not, but I had the same idea myself." Margot's quim dripped with anticipation. "How about if I wash down your back?" Margot winced inwardly at the too-obvious ploy.

"No, no, I think I'll get out. I feel much better now. I'll get Sweet Revenge lunged." Quickly, skirting Margot, Sally almost danced out of the shower.

As if she knew. Margot stared after her, almost in open-mouthed dismay. Of course Sally knew what Margot wanted. If Margot didn't want it, Margot would not have stepped inside the shower. She would have waited til Sally had finished. Why did Sally withhold her favors? Was she strictly a man's woman? Impossible. No one was. Did she belong to someone already? Unlikely.

Sally dressed and disappeared. Panting, almost feverish with desire, Margot leaned against the white tile wall and slowly dropped her fingers to her snatch, bulbous with desire, and rubbed it frantically, til she came in a pitiful imitation of sensuality.

Sally had made it clear. She wanted none of Margot. Her eyes were unsmilingly cold, her expression one of pained tolerance. She chatted and giggled with the others, but Margot—though it all belonged to her—was excluded. The pariah among the small group.

How ironic, she thought, as she trotted about the ring that afternoon and on into the evening, as Sally hosed down the just-ridden horses in the shower stall. I've fucked everyone here, except her. And I've never wanted to fuck anyone more than I've wanted her. How long would Sally stay under these conditions? When Sally left, Margot would probably be able to forget her, just as she forgot the others. But until then, she felt as if Sally paraded in front of her daily in a taunting flourish of daring sexuality.

Margot slowed the horse. Done, at last. It was 8:30. That had been a costly lunch. God, what a frustrating day, she thought. I'll see what Pete can give me.

The last embers of the blazing red sun were disappearing over the horizon as Margot stepped out of the barn, silent except for the occasional sounds of a cough, a slurped sip of water, an accidental kick on the door. Sally would be finished with night inspection, then initial the calendar to signify her presence. But Margot wouldn't wait. Sally had made it all too clear that she wasn't about to get involved. Margot steeled herself. She'd live. But while living, she was going to spend a hell of a long time trying to figure out what would entice Sally to her bed.

She trudged up the hill leading to the grooms' quarters. They lived in one large building, with separate entrances for each of the four suites. Each suite had a bedroom, living room, bathroom and efficiency kitchen, quite a good setup for these young grooms, some of them only eighteen, most never older than twenty five. For at twenty five, they usually decided to strike out on their own for the murky waters of possible success, or abandon horses altogether.

The white building seemed to gleam in the ever-darkening skies, as she passed by, bent on walking the long way to her home. She needed to stretch her legs, mull over her new client, think about High Flyer's difficulty with the triple combination jump. Blissfully, she rambled about her acres, watching isolated stars make their appearance as the night darkened and a sliver of a moon appeared.

At last, she turned back on the path, heading toward the grooms' quarters, toward her own farm house. Margot noticed a couple lights on in Pete's apartment, none in Corey or Craig's. One was on in Sally's. She glanced across the dirt road at her own home—an old farm house, built in the late 1860s with a porch that blocked the sun out of the lower floors, small rooms and giant fireplaces, crooked steps from the first floor to the second, an uneven second floor that made four-legged tables wobble uneasily if she pressed one corner.

Margot wiped her palms across her tight jeans and heaved a breath of anticipation. A good hearty roll in the hay with Pete. That's what she'd do tonight. It couldn't be much past nine or so. And she was sure he was still up, for she heard music wafting from the open screen window. She stopped. Oh hell, he wasn't alone. She wouldn't be able to fuck him after all, and no one else was about.

She bent slightly to peer into the window. Pete faced her, his arms locked around a girl, as they swayed—naked—to the soft tunes that Margot tried to recognize but couldn't. She felt herself grow wet as she watched him slide his hands down the girl's back to her buttocks and splay open the cheeks.

The girl leaned back, tilting her head, opening her mouth as if to kiss the air.

"Oh my God," Margot whispered, suddenly clutching at her chest for breath. Shock flew through her as she stared. For there was Sally in Pete's embrace. Sally, held and kissed and fondled by her own groom, the very man who held, kissed and fondled

31

her.

In desperation, Margot grabbed at the air, her fingers groping claws. She felt the air leave her body. But she could not move. Woodenly, she could only stare, open-mouthed, as they danced together, his knee pressing between her legs as they moved.

Pete, his long blond hair tied in a small pony tail at the nape of his neck, leaned forward and kissed Sally's full lips. Sally stretched her arms out and ran them down his face, across his smooth, muscular chest, down to his waist. She thrust her hips forward, even as he slid his leg still further between hers. Margot listened to them moan, as their fingers strolled over one another's bodies.

Margot slipped to her knees, shocked, blank. But, still, she couldn't turn her eyes away from the window.

Pete reached out and took Sally's perfect breasts in his hands, rotating them til Margot could hear her moan. Pete slid his fingers to their tips, tweaking the nipples til Sally writhed with delight. Sally dropped her hand to his crotch, taking his throbbing prick in her hand, rubbing it til it stood even more upright, a bulging club.

"Oh, God," Margot whispered, as Sally's buttocks danced enticingly to the music. Transfixed, she watched Pete slide his fingers between the cheeks of her ass, as his other fingers spread her cunt. Then, gently, he bent her over on all fours and came to stand behind her.

Sally was now on all fours, like the mares in the pastures. Pete was mounting her from behind like Rex, the Thoroughbred stallion. He reached around her and took her breasts in his hands, as she reached between his legs, fumbling for his balls and his cock. Then, finally, she pulled him toward her, pressing him to enter her inner depths.

Margot fell to her hands also, as if imitating Sally. But there was no passionate luxury. Instead, in frustration, she felt tears seep out of her eyes, as she clawed at the ground, grasping at the wooden floorboards, as wave after wave of shock and nausea and jealousy crashed through her.

Pete lunged against Sally, and she replied in kind. Their buttocks swayed together in joyous fulfillment. Finally, with a gasp of desire, they pushed a final, determined time and toppled in a heap of exhaustion on the hardwood floor of the apartment.

Margot managed to rouse herself only when she heard Sally and Pete bustling about. She had to get away. It wouldn't do if they found her, groveling on the ground in front of the window where they'd fucked. What did Sally want? Maybe Pete would know.

"Hullo, Pete?" she tilted her shoulder upward to grasp the phone under her ear as she made herself a cup of tea later that night. "Care to come over for a nightcap?" Would he? He generally wasn't good for more than a single fuck, but he'd never turned his boss down. So, perhaps, if pressed, he could get it up again.

"Uh, sure," he agreed without a moment's hesitation.

"Am I bothering you? I thought I saw your light on," she added sweetly. "Is someone there?"

"Nope. I'm alone. Be there in a couple minutes."

Pete hung up, as Margot walked around the oak kitchen, still brewing tea, still clutching the phone between ear and shoulder.

Good, she smiled to herself. That bitch is gone. Tomorrow I'll see what time she initialed her barn check. Tonight I'll get a little nooky. She replaced the receiver on the hook, gulped her tea and went to the front parlor to ready herself for Pete.

When she heard the light tap at the front door, she was ready. She'd top Sally any day. She opened the door, grinning broadly.

"Wow, Margot," Pete grinned in return, his full red cheeks puckering in admiration, as he stared.

For Margot was dressed as a cowgirl. Almost. She'd slipped off her panties and her jeans, and slipped on brown suede chaps that tightly curled around each long leg, and fastened together with a buckle at the waist. Her crotch and her bottom showed. Her breasts were bare, but for a sheriff's star she had hastily drawn around each nipple with her eye liner pencil.

"Come on in, pardner." Maybe Pete could only do it once, but he loved to dress up. He liked her in those crotchless panties and a tipless brassiere; in the harem costume with flowing chiffon handkerchiefs around her waist, in the black leather skirt and her knee-high black leather riding boots. Now this: suede chaps.

She sat down on a kitchen chair, opening her legs wide, and pushed herself forward. With contentment, she saw his eyes widen as he stared into her open snatch, fiery red and wet for him. All of a sudden, every passing frustration—from Sally with Eva at the restaurant to Ed Mason to Sally in the shower and Pete and Sally in the apartment crowded upon her. She didn't think she could wait for another moment without exploding.

"Take me, Pete," she whispered, reaching out for him. She grabbed at his belt and quickly, pulled it from the buckle.

Astonished, he stood before her, never taking his eyes from her beautiful, moist crotch, perched on the edge of the chair. He reached for her, feeling the wetness between his fingers. But Margot couldn't wait. Relentlessly, she unfastened his pants and roughly pulled them to the ground, even as she fumbled for his rod within his tight white jockey underwear.

"Oh, God," she sighed, "I need this. I need this so badly. Do it. Do it now. Hammer me."

"There's nothin' like you, Margot, nothin'," Pete responded, edging his flaccid member toward her opening.

For an answer, Margot pulled him to his knees so that they were eye to eye, organ to organ. "Do it," she commanded, "before I fire you!" She threw a leg over the arm of the chair, widening the dark chasm even more.

She waited impatiently as he hardened by watching her undulate her body. There was no romance here, she thought fleetingly and somewhat sadly. None of these guys held any romance. It was business. One horny fuck after the other. One thank you to Herbert after another. She reached for his cock and nimbly pressed her mouth to it, licking it til she felt the pulsations of his desire. Her other hand fingered her own mound restlessly waiting.

And then he was ready. Swiftly, manfully, he grasped Margot, bent to kiss her sheriff's stars, tweak them with his pliant fingers, as he shoved his member deep in her. She could scarcely await the penetration and rammed home against him til their spasm of lust ended.

Satiated, Margot fell back against the chair, eying his now-failing member contentedly. "What do you know about Sally?" She asked abruptly. She knew no other way.

"Well, you know her just as well as I do," he retorted, lying back on the kitchen floor, his head on his crossed arms.

"Does she screw?"

"Sure does." He winked.

"With you?"

"Yup. Why?"

"I wanted to make sure she wasn't lonely. If my grooms are lonely, then they leave. I don't like them to leave," Margot said matter-of-factly, trying to still her sudden trembling at the thought of that vivacious body. Then casually, almost as if an afterthought, she asked, "Is she any good?"

"Yeah."

Impatiently, Margot waited for more. But, even at his best, he was reticent, tight-lipped about virtually everything. "What do you mean?" Margot slid to the floor and ran her fingers over his blond brows and straight nose.

"Not as good as you, if that's what you mean."

"What do you mean?" she pressed.

"You know." But that was all he said. And she

knew him well enough to know that he would say no more, that he would be unable to articulate anything more.

She wanted Pete to tell her more about Sally, but if she asked too many questions, he'd know she wanted Sally and Sally would have none of her. That wasn't good for her reputation or her ego. And while it was true that Pete, Corey and Craig knew she screwed, they never talked about it. She knew that as certainly as she knew her name. She was off-limits for gossip.

"Who else does she screw?" Margot stood, pulling down the legs of her chaps til they clung smoothly to her body. He might think she was just casually gossiping.

"Corey, Craig, Eva over at Rob's place."

"Eva!" Margot exclaimed. So Sally balls everyone except me. Why not me? What's the matter with me? She clenched her fists together with a sudden ferocity that alarmed her. She wanted to race into Sally's room, pummel her awake and scream at her. I gave you this job, I am teaching you how to groom and train, and you fuck everyone else but me. Why?

Why?

What's so bad about me and so good about everyone else? She shrieked inwardly, baffled and tormented as panic almost crushed her. Would Sally never be hers?

CHAPTER 4

"Morning, Steven," Margot nodded almost perfunctorily as she stroke into the tack room where Steven was reattaching the reins to the snaffle bit.

"I wanted to switch bits. I've worked him on the flat. I thought I'd lighten him up with a twisted snaffle."

"Sounds logical. We'll concentrate on jumping." Margot poured herself another cup of black coffee. She peered through the window into the riding ring. "Who's that man holding the horse?" She was puzzled, not concerned.

"My dad." Steven laughed. "I guess you haven't met him. He's always in the office, working to pay for all of this." He shrugged, a devil-may-care shrug, implying that every eighteen-year-old was entitled to the luxuries of horses and grooms and trainers and thousand-dollar horse shows.

"I'd like to meet him." Margot turned on her heel and headed toward the tall, broad-shouldered man in the ring, holding High Flyer, one of his son's two horses.

"Hello. I'm Margot. You're Steven's father?"

The man turned toward her, his iron-gray hair dropping casually into his forehead. His square jaw jutted forward, bespeaking power. Deep almost-black eyes under thick iron-gray eyebrows seemed to cut through her. Beneath his suit and starched white shirt and tie Margot spied a broad chest, powerful arms. His son looked just like him.

"Hello, Margot. I'm pleased to meet you." His

mellifluously deep voice wafted over her in comfortable waves of kindness and, surprisingly, titillation. "I'm Malcolm Forsythe."

"I'm sorry I've not met you before," Margot found herself blushing as their hands clapsed in greeting. "I'm glad you'll see him ride."

"I've seen him at some of his horse shows. Not all, I'm afraid. His mother usually accompanies him. But I'll be around for some time, and I'd like to watch his development as he nears the high-stakes shows of the season." He smiled, almost apologetically. "I'm no rider, but I appreciate the sport. Actually, any sport."

She felt his eyes bore through her, strip her, and she shifted with embarrassment. "What do you like about sports so much?" She bent down, fastening the wide elastic band that clipped her blue jeans under her paddock boots so they wouldn't rise up, wrinkle and cut her with saddle sores when she rode.

"Discipline. Discipline is critical to success in life. I want Steven to learn that lesson well. And I think he's on his way," he replied roughly, as his son walked through the door, reins and bit in hand.

How ferocious, Margot thought quickly. Not at all like Steven. Steven was soft and gentle. He was focused and disciplined—riding every day for several hours—but he was not filled with the ferocity of his father. "Why don't you step into the office. There are some chairs and you can watch through the window. We don't want you getting trampled."

Steven refastened the bridal and jumped onto his horse.

"I'd like to watch from the ring. If I stand next to

39

you I don't suppose I'll be trampled," he replied, adjusting his tie tighter to his throat.

"I'm sorry," she spoke softly, through gritted teeth. "That is against rules."

"Whose rules are they?"

"Mine, Mr. Forsythe. I find my students don't concentrate if someone else is in the arena."

"Rules are made to be broken," he answered firmly.

"Not here, Mr. Forsythe." Margot didn't budge.

"Wherever they need to be."

She looked up, for he was fully eight inches taller, and placed her hands on her hips. "I'm afraid I won't be able to start this lesson until you have left the ring."

Margot heard Steven shift uncomfortably on the back of his horse. Vaguely she wondered if he was used to these confrontations. She also wondered what the expected outcome usually was. For she was not one to be crossed. Nor, it seemed, was Malcolm.

Malcolm glared at her. "What do you do that is so private, if I may venture to ask." His voice grew steely, his eyes hard.

"We concentrate. Discipline. The values you admire. I don't want Steven thinking about you. I want him thinking about his horse and about me." Margot's eyes flashed in anger and impatience. She heard the grooms at the doorway, listening and watching. For people didn't defy her. She rarely met her match. It was well-known in this horse world that what Margot wanted, Margot got.

"That, my dear girl, may be the problem."

"What?" she snarled. "If you care to watch his

40

lessons from the center of the ring, find another trainer. If you care to have Steven go home with you, then feel free to stand in the middle of the ring. But I'm running out of time for your stupidity."

Sally gasped. Margot turned on her heel and headed out the door.

"Margot," Sally whispered, grabbing her sleeve. "Do you know who that is?" Without waiting for a reply, Sally burst forth. "He's the chairman of the Forsythe Foundation. You know, the largest charitable foundation in the country. Their family is centuries old, their money is older, and he's one of the most powerful people in America." Sally snickered. "And you just told him to drop dead." She peered at Margot admiringly.

Any other time, Margot would have lapped up the attention, would have focused on the newest twist in her flirtation with Sally, but not now. Fury blinded her. The audacity of that man to think he could run this place as he probably ran every other place.

"Dad," she could hear Steven's pleading voice. "Dad," he repeated. She imagined that he leaned down from the horse, his fingers gripping his father's shoulder, tugging at him like a little boy, begging him to leave.

Margot's chest heaved in exhaustion. And then, when she heard Malcolm's tread behind her, heaved in exhilaration.

"Our interchange has not ended," he whispered into her ear, his hot breath searing her.

Margot froze, her shoulders tightening, her hands clenching spasmodically as an unwelcome surge of heat coursed through her. "Is that so?" she replied archly, without turning. She waited, hands by her side, until she heard his departing steps.

"I'll bet Steven's days are numbered with you, Margot," Sally whispered fearfully.

"I'll not be bossed around my own farm." Margot's lips were as pale as her cheeks, from the exertion of the exchange and the unexpected passion of the moment. But she pulled herself upright. For it wouldn't do for her staff to see that she felt debilitated by her encounter. Margot the Strong must not falter. "Now, let's get on with the lesson," she said thickly, turning and walking back into the arena.

"Margot, Margot I'm sorry," Steven stood holding his horse by the reins. "My dad is used to getting his way. He came to see me ride, and I guess he didn't want a window between him and—and you. And me," he added quickly, dropping his eyes as if in shame. "He thought you were really great looking."

Margot's chest swelled, as a sudden deluge of tears threatened. Was Malcolm Forsythe *flirting?* He certainly went about it strangely. Maybe not, she mused. Maybe in his world, power said it all. If you were powerful and bossy, everyone thought you were sexy and gorgeous. He may have thought she was attractive, but he challenged her in a way she didn't like.

"Let's get on with it, then," she smiled, her voice brisk in an effort to hide the conflicting, competing emotions that pulled at her. For she thought he, too, was good-looking.

But her mind was not on High Flyer or Steven or the placement of his hands and legs. She pondered, instead, the strings tugging fiercely at her. Sally. And now Malcolm. Goddamn it! Would there never be any peace?

She didn't welcome the flashing light on her message machine when she stopped home for lunch. Today it seemed like an infringement. If someone wanted her, he should call her at the barn. Reluctantly, she played back the message. It was Herbert, inviting her for dinner with him and Ed Mason, in town for a few days. Reluctantly, she returned the call, and agreed to be ready at seven, when Herbert would call for her.

But that wasn't what she wanted at all. She didn't want polite conversation with Herbert and her new customer, Ed Mason. What she really wanted was a good lay with Craig. She didn't want to do business tonight. She wanted to forget business.

Craig always made it fun. Corey liked to lie about on the bed, Pete liked masquerading, and Craig liked to frolic.

She smiled now as she showered under the steaming water. Just last week, Craig hid in a large pile of loose hay, lonesome strands that had been swept together. She heard his voice calling to her, and then she dug about to uncover him. She found him, entirely dressed, for the hay was prickly, except for his manhood, standing bolt upright. His purple-veined hard-on beckoned, and without waiting, Margot dove in, quickly pulling down her jeans so she could sit down on him. He reached under her cotton shirt, found her breasts within their lacy constraints and toyed with them til she moaned with joy, even as she and Craig plunged against one another in the hay pile. He flirted. He'd bring her to the brink, hear her moans, feel her force, then withdraw, leaving her high and dry, lurching with terrible angst. Then he'd begin again, take her bit by bit, then leave her stranded. Finally, he'd cross the passionate threshold.

Now Margot drew the lather through her hair, lifting it section by section onto her head into luxurious piles. Then, the water pelting down, she stepped back underneath the shower faucet, washing out the soap. Only the sound of the bathroom door opening roused her. Anger replaced her initial fear. Who would have the audacity to barge in? She peered through the mottled glass of the shower door, and smiled benignly.

For there stood Herbert with the *droit du seigneur*. He bought this place for her. He could screw her when he wanted. Herbert stripped off his clothes, his prick already rising and stepped in to join her. Vaguely, as Margot turned the water to its full force, to spray out over the entire square they occupied, did she wonder if he thought she waited for him and only him. Probably not. But he didn't want to know who else she screwed. He was very careful to call first, very careful to avoid an embarrassing scene.

Margot smiled, opening her mouth to welcome the raindrops. She bent to her knees, her mouth still open, and took him. As she sucked him, she took her thick hair, still soapy and soggy, and ran it under his scrotom, through his legs to his ass. He gasped as its silken feel seemed to strangle him, even as her tongue played with the end of his cock.

Margot watched his toes curl and uncurl spasmodically, as she deftly addressed him til he grew as hard

44

as a wooden mallet. With her hair like a vice, she pulled him to the tile floor and faced him, her legs clasped about his hips. She leaned forward to kiss him and felt his tongue enter her mouth, his fingers touch her breasts in deep caresses. His cock played with the outer folds of her quim.

Herbert urged her backward, stretching her out til she lay open before him. Her hair released him. He leaned down, taking her mound in his mouth. His tongue darted within the soft folds of skin, tousseling with her desire, as his fingers reached for her breasts, his lips for hers, while the water played upon their bodies. Margot groaned, wrapped her legs about his strong, wide back as he entered her. She ran her fingers through his thick white hair, matted with water.

At last he stopped and sat up. "Sit here," he whispered. Silently, she obeyed, tossing her luxuriant hair over his shoulders. The soap peeled off her in great streaks, covering him in white lather also, as their bodies slipped and slid together in full release.

"I probably don't have enough pressure in the pump for this," she giggled, extracting herself from his body.

"I have to take short showers in this old farm house. You'll have to put in a new pump." She kissed him familiarly on his white-haired chest.

"What's the matter with my pump?" He pouted, dropping his eyes to his member in jest. He tipped her head back and kissed her neck and shoulders and lips.

At last Margot stood, and put out a hand to help him stumble to his feet in the tiny square shower.

"Hell, Margot, on second thought, you can afford a new pump. This place makes a lot of money," he retorted gruffly. "I knew you and it were a good investment."

"In more ways than one," she stretched her hand out and patted his member. "Let's go. I'm starving."

Now for the hard part, she thought glumly. Business conversation. Ed'll want to know how I got into horses and then I'll tell him about the 4-H club and my first pony that we purchased for five hundred dollars, which also included three months board and the bridle and saddle. I'll tell him how I'd get thrown ten times a day by the pony in those first months, but by autumn's end had it perfectly trained.

She sighed. She supposed all this talk was part of business, but she sure wished all she had to do was ride silently, and not bother with this salesmanship. She pulled a loose cotton denim dress over her white lace demi-bra and white silk bikini panties. She drew a large black velvet elastic over her hair, tying it at the nape of her neck. Behind her, she heard Herbert stuffing his feet into his brown loafers.

Then she'd tell Ed, as she told countless other customers, that she spent every day after school and all vacations working with James Caruthers, one of the world's best-known trainers, learning everything about horses. She giggled, remembering him. He hadn't been interested in her. Just men. She hadn't known that when she wandered into the office late one night, searching for a pen.

There he was bent over the desk, and another man, unknown to her, was behind him. Their pants were down about their ankles as the stranger pumped her boss. She didn't need more than a startled glance to know exactly what they were about. Terrified, she'd backed out, apologizing and blushing. For though it hadn't been her fault, she knew her career was over. She wouldn't be easily forgiven for that. She raced back to the stalls and stood, trembling, not knowing how she'd ever face him again.

But when he left the office awhile later and found her, still shaking, clutching at a bar on a stall door, he'd soothingly told her there was nothing to be embarrassed about. But he pressed her. Was she embarrassed because she'd walked in on the sexual act, or because the act was with a man? She hesitated, not yet knowing. And she didn't know, not for months. For she was still so young and innocent. She'd only had her boyfriend.

And then he'd asked her again, one autumn afternoon as they rode two quarter horses on a trail through the mountains. By then she didn't have her one and only boyfriend, but she'd found ample replacements in her new friends, Becky, Cathy, Bill. And none of it seemed strange anymore. Anything Jim wanted to do was fine. She knew she'd never blush again. Never.

Then she joined Walt. But at last, at twenty four, she knew she was ready for her own farm. She grinned to herself. It was one thing to know you were ready to own a farm and be a trainer. It was another finding someone to help you do it.

She knew, for her story was well-rehearsed that there were only certain things she could tell customers. She would tell Ed about her national prominence as a trainer and rider, and how she met

Herbert at a show just when she was scouting about for a backer, and he was scouting about for an investment. It was a tidy little package—especially for a divorced rich man.

"Which perfume should I use?" she asked Herbert teasingly as he walked out of the bathroom and found her still in front of the mirror over the bureau.

"The one with the bow." He cupped his hands on her rounded breasts as she lifted her arms to dab a bit of Cabochard perfume from the bottle with the glass bow onto the pulses of her neck. She felt a surge of excitement, as he tweaked her nipples with his fingers.

"Herbert," she breathed, "aren't we going to be late?" The tingling became invasive.

"Hardly," he leaned forward, his breath in her ear. She pressed her thighs together, as the tingling swelled through her. "He'll understand, I'm sure." Herbert did not relinquish her breasts, as he massaged them and tweaked their ends.

"Oh, God, Herbert," Margot breathed, a flush of desire spreading through her. Unthinking, she began swaying her hips in a fine, undulating motion. She reached behind her and pulled his shaft, thick and throbbing, from his pants. She hiked her dress and dropped her silk panties to the floor, and reached for him, pulling him by his prick to the front of her.

He never released his hold on her heaving breasts. The swell of desire overpowered them, and she pulled him into her waiting cavity. But he stopped, the tip of his member teasing the outer folds of her cavities.

"Herbert," Margot wailed. "Don't stop. Do it,

48

now."

But Herbert merely dipped inside of her quickly, flirtatiously, as Margot arched forward and back with hearty lust. She wailed, calling his name, reaching for him, her arms stretched out in a pleading gesture. "Herbert, please." She almost wept with despair. But finally, he came to her again, feeding the fires that he had ignited.

"We better hurry," Herbert at last muttered, replacing his now softened member in his pants, and glancing at the clock on the bed table. "You always make me late because you're too attractive," he jokingly chided her.

"Well, we won't let on why we're late." Margot tossed her hair over her shoulders as they closed the screen door behind them to meet Ed Mason for dinner.

CHAPTER 5

"He made me laugh," she said aloud to no one as she danced around her bedroom with the brass bedframe, the oak armoire and night tables and bureau with the white porcelain knobs.

"And I haven't laughed in ages." Business took its toll. Training Steven and the two others, training fifteen horses, yearning for Sally. But Ed Mason had made her laugh. He was witty and charming and delightful. And when dinner at Herbert's was over, he drove her home, walked her to the door, and in a rather old-fashioned way, kissed her lightly on the cheek and thanked her for a most enjoyable evening.

Margot plopped down on her bed cross-legged. "Oh, lordy, but that was good," Margot said aloud. For they had laughed about commercials and movie stars, horseback riders and government leaders. Never had the mundane looked more fanciful and delectable. Never had she felt more alive and sensational. "Oh, Ed Mason, you are as wonderful as you always seemed to be on television."

Margot reached for the small bottle of red nailpolish on the night table next to her bed, kicked off her beige sandals and delicately polished her toenails til the layers gleamed and sparkled in a lacquer. She twirled her feet, humming as she reconsidered her delicious night with that exceptional newscaster.

And she waited impatiently for his call. When she returned from the barn, she immediately glanced at the answering machine in hopes that its blinking light signified his call. When she arrived at the barn after an absence, she'd immediately scan the messages for one from him. But so far, there'd been nothing. So far, no message on the machine, no message scribbled on the pink memo pads from a groom.

There was a call about more hay from Will, another about shoeing from the farrier, Lincoln. The vet had phoned about worming the horses, Rob had called inviting her out for pizza, Richard had invited her to the movies, Andrea had called from Hudson to see if she wanted to get together. But no Ed. She even had a call from Larry McIntosh whom she hadn't spoken to in months. But no Ed.

Now, Margot stamped her foot impatiently. She

supposed she should call him, but he seemed decidedly too old-fashioned for that. And he was probably too famous. Too many women probably pursued him. So she'd wait. She made some lemonade and settled herself on the front porch on the white wicker rocking chair, watching the last remnants of the sun. At the very least she ought to return her phone calls. But, no, not tonight. It was too tranquil.

She squinted, for in the distance, the lone figure of Sally was making her way toward the house. Idly, she watched Sally's hips sway, her long legs swathed in tight faded jeans stretch one before the other. As she drew closer, Margot watched her pert breasts under the tight white T-shirt. Margot squeezed her legs together. God, even as I sit here hoping Ed will call, the sight of Sally makes me hot. She waved languidly.

"Want some lemonade?" she offered as Sally climbed the two steps to the porch and leaned against the railing.

"No thanks. I just wanted to talk," she said smiling that wide smile that seemed to show all her gleaming white, even teeth.

"Oh?" Margot raised her brows nervously. Did she want more money? Was she quitting? Did she come to ask Margot to make love to her? Which tack would Sally take, and could she stop her if it were the wrong one?

"Look Margot," Sally began, running her fingers through her unruly red hair that just covered her ears. "I've been here ten months, I've ridden all my life. But I want to start training."

Margot swallowed. So that was it. She wanted to

become a trainer now, immediately. Like all the other girls, she didn't want to wait, didn't want to put in her time and learn how to train. She just wanted to jump on the horse and take off and call herself a trainer.

"Oh?" she merely said, her voice even and expressionless. Sally, after all, was as bad as the rest of the overeager, ridiculous girls and boys who groomed for her.

"I want you to teach me how to train."

"I am. What do you think I'm doing when I ask you to lunge a horse? When I ask you to put draw reins on him and work him from the ground?"

"I don't want to do it from the ground, and then let you do the work on his back. I want to ride them now. I want you to give me a horse to train from scratch. I can do it. Of course, I'll continue with all my regular duties, but I want just one horse to teach to jump properly." Sally clasped her hands in front of her, drawing her firm breasts together in enticing curves.

Margot eyed her closely, seeing the urgency in her face. She took a sip of lemonade, studying the situation. She should fire her, just as she'd fired the others who'd ask for this privilege well before their time. You couldn't work ten months and think you understood the business, at least not on Margot's level, and Margot didn't want to be associated with poorly trained horses. She didn't want to be known as a trainer who'd lightly let others begin to mold her horses.

She bit her lip. It was time to tell Sally she was weak-kneed and too dumb to know she didn't begin to understand how to train a superior horse. It was time to tell her she was fired. For now that Sally had made the request, Margot knew she'd become too impetuous and too aggressive to patiently serve her.

"Not yet, Sally," she merely said, her heart thumping, for she knew she'd erred. Fire her, her good sense told herself. "You need to watch me more, you need to work them on the ground more." She tried to keep her voice hard and coarse, but it was soft and soothing. Fire her, Margot. But she couldn't. She could not possibly see the last of Sally.

"How long?" Sally begged, her brows knitting together, her blue eyes flashing with eagerness. "What happens if I buy my own horse and train it? Is that proof?"

Margot shrugged. "It might be the proof you need to go out on your own, but it won't necessarily be the proof I need to let you train my horses. Look, Sally," Margot placed her glass on the ground and leaned forward, stopping the rocker with the tip of her bare foot. "Anyone can hang a shingle and call herself a trainer and make a horse rideable. But that's not the business I'm in. Your horse might not be good enough for me."

"I want to be a trainer," Sally said, emphasizing each word evenly.

"You mean you like the sound of the title, 'trainer?'"

"Yes, partly. And I'd like the thrill of training."

Margot released the rocker with her toe, settling back against the wicker. She supposed she could let Sally call herself Assistant Trainer and let her have a horse, under Margot's close scrutiny. But the others — Corey, Craig and Pete who'd been here longer — would be furious. Then she'd have a free-for-all, and they'd all quit. True, Sally was the best damn groom she'd ever had: fast, thorough, earnest. But it wouldn't fly to give her that privilege. And once she had the privilege, you could bet your last buck that she wouldn't want to muck out stalls and cool down horses anymore.

"Look, Margot, I'm gonna get a horse. There's one for sale. Can I train him? Will you give me an empty stall in the outer barn?" Sally leaned forward, so that only the tip of her buttocks touched the railing. Her eyes bore into Margot's.

That would certainly give Margot an excuse to award Sally that coveted role of Assistant Trainer. God, she didn't want Sally to leave. She was too good — and too desirable. But she would leave if she weren't rewarded. On the other hand, if she were rewarded with Assistant Trainer too soon, she'd also leave as a cocky, self-assured trainer. No, Margot bit her lip. Maybe if she held out, Sally would come to her again in several more months.

Or better yet — Margot beamed, for she'd hit upon an idea — Sally would come to her with another offer, one that had nothing to do with horses. A sort of physical bribe, and Margot would see her way clear.

"Buy yourself that horse, then, as a first step," she rasped, placing her hand on her heart to still its urgent beating. She longed to pull Sally toward her, embrace her, place her lips on Sally's, and then kiss every inch of her delightful body.

"Great!" Sally jumped up and clapped her hands. "I'll be back tomorrow with Thad."

"Thad? Hadn't you better get a more elegant name?" Margot half way snorted.

"When he's elegant, then I'll rename him," Sally laughingly rejoined as she stepped off the porch. "I've got to run. Pete invited me for TV dinner!" She waved and in a burst of delight, sped across the dirt road and the field, heading back toward the grooms' quarters.

Margot stared after her, bereft. Sally's life was so full of anticipation. A horse, a tangible future, dinner, television and a man. And she didn't give a damn about Margot. Did it dawn on Sally that if she bedded Margot, her future might be assured here? Or did she have so much faith in her ability and her attractiveness, that she didn't think she'd have to bribe anyone?

Margot sighed as if to wipe away the heaviness that settled on her insides, like leaden weights pulling her down. She stared into the darkness. Just a stripe of orange remained on the horizon. Everyone was going off with someone tonight. Sally to Pete, Ed to someone. Herbert to someone. Even the sun was going away.

It wasn't as if she didn't have a future, but it was harder and less clear, because the stakes were higher. And then there was that problem with Steven's father, Malcolm Forsythe.

The preemptory letter. She swallowed, trying to put it out of her mind. It was abrupt, regal and businesslike. It was an ill omen hanging above her, the albatross threatening. She hadn't done anything about it, except stuff it in the top drawer of her desk in the office. But it was there, had been there for several days.

Abruptly, Margot stood, absently kicking over the almost full glass of lemonade. She'd better review that letter again, to gauge exactly where her future was going, what, precisely, she could do about it, whether it was too late, in fact, to do anything about it.

For something gnawed at her, telling her that letter had already spelled her doom. The fact that he wanted to speak to her did not bode well. Margot grimaced as she reached for the lemonade glass. She stomped inside, throwing the screen door so far open behind her that even she started when it closed with a ferocious bang.

She turned toward her living room, and stopped. She eyed the two couches with their small red, white and green floral prints and the two side chairs with other red, white and green flora. But she was unable to ignore the activities that she knew didn't include her. She dropped to her knees on the couch by the window and peered out of the panes of glass. In the distance she saw the lights in the grooms' quarters. She thought she detected music wafting over the pastures.

Margot winced.

CHAPTER 6

Herbert was away, his secretary informed Margot the following day. Not expected to return for several weeks. Her heart lunged, for he was on one of the islands in the Caribbean, rather unreachable. It was mean of him not to tell her when he was off, but he'd always behaved that way and she could usually shrug it off philosophically. Not now though.

She had determined that she must speak to him about the letter, the ominous sounding letter.

But suddenly it was too late. For Malcom Forsythe left a curt message on the machine in the barn office. He didn't tell her to call him. Nor did he say he'd call back. He merely said he'd called. She felt as if he were stalking her, trying to rattle her til she quivered and apologized and slunk back to him. Is that how corporate takeovers and mergers were accomplished? She wondered, smiling feebly to herself. Well, I'm one company that will give you quite a proxy fight. But she felt rather tremulous at the thought of taking him on. It might cost her a lot.

She wouldn't tell Steven, for she knew this would upset him, and he had an important show in two days, a show that might, if he performed well, garner him the last McClay win be needed to qualify for the Regionals. No, she'd let it be. Perhaps she'd see Malcolm at the show, perhaps he'd come to see his son ride.

Still, despite her decisions, she felt weighed down, on edge: Malcolm plagued her. Sally plagued her. Ed's absence plagued her.

And, then suddenly, she heard the office door open. And there, in front of her, stood Ed, grinning affably. "I brought my horse. He's in the trailer." His tall, wiry frame stood before her, a welcome, gratifying sight.

At least one thing was going right, she muttered to herself. Ed, at last.

"You did?" she gasped. "Why didn't you call? I wasn't expecting you."

"Did enough inquiring about you to know that I wanted to have at least one of them here, and that I wanted to see if you were free for dinner."

Margot jumped up, as if that leaden weight that had dragged her downward for days, had been tossed off. "You bet," she giggled. "But first things first." She placed her finger on the intercom, paging Pete. "Help me unload that horse in the trailer, Pete. And ask Corey or Craig to fix up stall number three. Check the bedding, hay and water." She turned, wiping the perspiration off her brow. Silly how Ed's presence could change it all for her.

"Let's go," she beamed.

Carefully, she lifted the back off the navy two-horse trailer, and unfastened the chain that blocked the Warmblood's movements.

"Whoa," she called softly as she climbed on and unfastened the lines that held the horse. Then carefully, she backed him down the ramp toward Pete, waiting at the bottom.

"Why don't you walk him a bit, Pete?" She handed her groom the leadline. Did he fuck Sally nightly? How did they compare?

Smiling, she turned toward Ed. Well, then, I'll

fuck you instead. Sally won't be the only one who gets a little sex tonight. "He'll take care of the horse. Come, tell me about him, sign some papers, and then let's have dinner."

This time, when he dropped Margot at her screen door, she invited him in. She prepared some tea and sat down on the couch next to him in the living room. Only the soft light of the hurricane lamp next to her cast a quiet haze about the room. But they didn't say much as the teabags steeped in the china pot before them.

Margot shivered, despite the summer night, as Ed wrapped his long arm about her and drew her close to him.

"I've wanted to do this since I met you," he murmured into her ear.

His lips dropped to her lobes as he casually nibbled at them. She felt herself grow weak at his touch and lay against his arm, unmoving, as the pit of her stomach churned with anticipation. His fingers drifted to her white cotton blouse, fumbled for the buttons, then dipped into her white lace bra to knead the swell of her soft breasts. Margot moved her hips, trying to twist toward him to press herself against him.

Ed's fingers dropped forward til they found the taut tips of her breasts. With one sweeping brush, he dropped her white cotton shirt and bra straps to her arms, exposing her beautiful breasts to the low lamplight. His mouth dropped to the ends as he suckled them, even as his fingers fumbled with the clasp of her pants.

Margot didn't move as waves of desire surged

through her. She glanced down at his pants, detecting a ripple of hardening flesh within, but she did nothing more than open her legs, feeling the moisture gathering between them as he deliberately aroused her.

He grunted, as he pulled her pants down. Squirming, as Ed now played with the opening of her cavity, Margot freed herself of all her clothes and sat, naked before him, an exotic pearly lustre in the lamplight. His lips covered her face with kisses, his hands roamed freely over the curves and swells of her body as desire swept through her.

She smiled to herself, pleased with the effect her nakedness had on this man. His eyes widened with unadulterated joy, his breath came more quickly, more heavily as he drank in her pale body, wrapped in the long folds of her ebony hair. She listened to him moan with appreciation, as he loosened his gentle hold on her and sat back against the couch, just to admire the flesh before him.

"Now what?" she murmured, lifting his long fingers to her lips. She longed to take him.

She ran her tongue along the sides, then nibbled the soft skin at the tips. But only for a moment, for he withdrew his fingers and placed both hands firmly on her breasts, massaging them, urging her backward against the couch as he explored her body.

Vaguely, she thought how strange it felt to be the recipient. Usually, she was the aggressor, the one to pull at the zipper, snatch the bulging member from its underwear, put her lips and palm to it. But not here, not today. And she acquiesced—mesmerized by him.

Then Ed lifted her hand and placed it on a button of his shirt. His signal that she was to perform at last. Margot reached out, unfastening Ed's dark plaid shirt to reveal his wide, tanned chest, with a trail of brown hair down the center.

She closed her eyes and pulled at his belt, then the pants button, then the zipper. Surprisingly, his pants slid apart easily, no strain against material that had grown suddenly too tight with sexual adventures. How could this be? Alarmed, she peered at him, almost soft. Why? Surely, he had seemed enraptured moments ago when he gazed at her. Surely, he eagerly caressed her breasts.

Puzzled, she tentatively reached out for him, placing her hand on the soft flesh before her. What was going on? In all her years of experience, this had not occurred before. It was she who usually slowed the fire-breathing man down, pushed him away so he could cool off. But now? She pressed her hand firmly against him, then extricated his failing, flopping member from his underwear.

She glanced upward, but he seemed oblivious to her consternation, as his hands gently enveloped her breasts. With both hands, she reached out, and placed his prick between her palms, rolling him like bread dough, willing him to harden. What was the matter with her? She dropped her fingers to his scrotom, but even this failed to help. It couldn't be her. What was the matter with *him*?

"Margot, don't worry," he whispered. "Roll over. I want to see your ass." Ed stood, kicking his clothes to the ground.

He was so tall, and his penis was so long and

lanky. It reminded her of a bath toy bobbing around in the clear water, or a rubber mouse filled with cat-nip that the cat tossed about with his front paws. She would have laughed, had she not felt embarrassed for him and perplexed. She was no longer hot and frazzled as she had been minutes before. She was merely curious and annoyed.

"Roll over," he whispered, giving her a slight jolt.

Obediently, Margot rolled over, pushing her firm, round buttocks in the air, slightly parting her legs. He patted them, gently at first, then a little harder. She wiggled. It was surprisingly arousing.

Again, he hit her, this time a resounding, noisy slap. Margot shifted, wiggling her backside in the response she thought he expected. He didn't hurt her, but he surprised her. Is *this* what made him hard? Doing it up the butt? But that, for her, was off limits. She turned her head to tell him she didn't do it that way. But it seemed rather pointless, for even as he bent over her, he remained useless to her.

And then suddenly, a loud swat clouded her thoughts, as his giant hand slammed against her left cheek, then her right. The sting froze her. He swat-ted both cheeks again.

"Oh, don't," she breathed, angrily, jerking her head backward to rebuke him soundly. But she could merely drop her jaw wide in admiration. For his member had suddenly risen upright, firm, pulsating with throbbing, purple veins. He was long and thick, as nothing she had ever seen.

"Oh, wow," she repeated, softly in wonder. Sud-denly, she found herself squirming with desire at the sight of him, even though she knew she would not accept his rear entry. She reached her arm backward, longing to touch him. But he stepped back. Clearly, he would have none of that. What, then *would* he have? She thought she'd explode.

Another smack roused her from the hot lethargy she had drifted toward. She squirmed, this time to try to stop the blows. But he reached out, grabbing her two hands that she'd placed against the arms of the couch to push herself upright. He held them, squeezing her wrists tightly, as his other hand hit her cheeks in rhythm. The left, the right.

She arched upright, wiggled to either side as he seemed to split her in half with his violence. "Stop, stop, Ed," she pleaded, her voice catching in her throat, tears of anguish falling down her cheeks. She writhed, further incensing him as he increased the speed and the force of the blows he rained upon her backside.

Margot gritted her teeth, squeezing her eyes shut. It can't last forever she said, tightening every muscle in her body as again and again he assailed her. Would he never stop? Would he kill her? Wouldn't getting it up the butt have been preferable? But, she reminded herself quickly, she'd never had a choice.

"How do you like this?" he breathed roughly, even as he slapped her. "Hot? Does it make you hot? It does for me. I don't want to hurt you, really I don't. Margot. I don't, I don't," he repeated almost savagely, faster and faster as the slaps fell upon her with greater speed and urgency. And then, as abruptly as he started, he stopped and fell upon her, separating her legs, entering her cavity—no longer moist with longing—from behind. He groaned, grabbing at her shoulders, humping her. Grunting, he pushed against her frantically til at last he stopped and lay still, panting heavily.

"Get off," Margot's voice was muffled by the pillows on the couch. "How dare you do that?" With her legs, she kicked at him, til he rolled off and slid to the floor, his cock still hard.

He sat up against the couch, legs bent, hands resting easily on his knees. He smiled contentedly, gazing into the empty fireplace.

"How dare you?" She seethed indignantly. She turned her head to see the sides of her buttocks. Red, shockingly bright red. "How *could* you?" she moaned, rubbing them with her hands. The confidence she'd always felt evaporated. The joy in which she'd always enveloped herself ebbed.

"Get out," she said dully. "Just get out."

I can't believe what I have just let him to do me, she thought. I am a numbskull to have accepted it. Vaguely, she wondered if she could have escaped him. Surely, she could have been strong enough to pull herself free, or to have thrust her leg outward to kick him. Angrily, she shook her head. She had lost control with him.

"You haven't done this before?" he asked, his voice registering surprise. Then, he reached up, laying a hand lightly on her buttocks. "They're red. They must hurt. Let me get you something."

"Don't touch me," she said bitterly, through gritted teeth. Bitter, because she had hoped for so much. Bitter, because she had been so sorely hurt. Bitter because she had *let* him.

He stood and trundled off to the kitchen, whistling

slightly between his teeth. Margot buried her face in her hands. The sting and the humiliation were unbearable. How could she face a man like this again and hope to be respected? Then she felt his gentle touch and the cooling, soothing cold towels on her backside, smoothing away the pain. He bent over, kissing her tenderly on the neck.

Tears welled in her eyes. He was so gentle now, so violent before. "Don't do this," she said. "Get out of my house. Just get out." She flung her arm back, striking his chest. "Get out of my house." She forced herself to stand, throwing him backward.

She grabbed the arm of the couch to steady herself as pain stung her again. Then, bending painfully, she reached for his clothes and unsteadily made her way to the door. She tossed them on the porch. "Get out of my house now. Or I shall call the sheriff."

Heaving, she fell back against the door jamb watching Ed stand.

"I'm surprised, really surprised," he said.

Margot slammed the door behind him and for the first time, she locked it. Her heart hammering, she leaned back, resting her body on the wall, waiting for the pain that wracked her entire body to subside.

She turned off the outside light and the hall light, so it was dark outside. Then squinting, she peered out the long glass window on the side of the door, seeing him awkwardly stoop to pick up his clothes, then, hopping, lift each leg into his pants. He didn't look sexy or manful anymore. He looked like a tall, skinny guy getting dressed in the dark.

But Margot couldn't stop thinking about him as the next day passed. Angrily, she tossed her head, wondering why she permitted him to beat her. And every time she thought of him, a flush of heat would pass through her. It was bizarre, she thought idly, moving her pinky fingers to release the reins just a bit. Maybe, she was just curious to see precisely what it took to arouse Ed, and then, she was curious to see what this form of foreplay was really like.

She pressed her legs into the horse's flank to bring his hind end under. Maybe, just maybe, she mused, she even, sort of, *liked* it. For today, as she thought about it, a flush of desire would pass through her.

As Margot worked Ed's horse, standing in the center of the ring and lunging the horse on a long line, moving about her in a circle, she imagined his master's lean body, his lanky soft cock and the lanky hard one that pummeled her. She felt that welcome tingle gather at her center, the one that had been sorely lacking last night.

"God, I'm horny," she muttered, "Why? After that beating I should probably never think of him or sex again." But the strange sensation of intense longing swelled through her as she rode her horses and taught her students.

CHAPTER 7

Margot pursed her lips, narrowing her eyes. Steven would ride next. The course was complicated, the competition difficult. She'd reviewed the speed at which he needed to ride to keep the proper strides between the fences. She glanced at him, but he was busy studying the course.

He looked dapper, one of the few males riding. Mostly girls rode. But, oddly enough, she mused, at the very top reaches of the spot, it was the men who were most successful. Probably because their strength enabled them, ultimately, to muscle the horse over the five or six foot jumps.

Steven's velvet huntcap almost glinted in the sunlight, his navy pinstripe jacket and beige pants sparkled with fresh pressing and cleaning. His tie was centered down his white Oxford shirt. This year, he was the prize student. Next year, she would have Marcy and Jenny to compete for these highest honors. They just needed a bit more experience and then they, too, would be ready. It would be convenient, for Steven would have become too old to be eligible for these competitions.

Steven smiled nervously as the previous rider ended her course, and he softly kicked his horse.

"You're terrific, Steven. You know it all," Margot said, brushing her hand across his thigh, pressed against his horse's flank.

She turned back toward the ring, eying the spectators gathered around the pristine white fence. Behind them, a soft hill with the green of summer rolled into distant trees and pastures and white houses.

The soft noise of people chattering as they watched the equitation ring where Steven would now ride to show off his best form, or the hunt course, where he had ridden earlier to show off his horse's best form, was lulling. But it was a false sense of lull, for Steven faced a critically important ride now. Behind her other horses, their riders mounted on their backs, milled about either waiting for their turn or waiting for results of this key competition.

Steven executed a perfectly formed circle and then asked High Flyer to canter on the left lead. The horse began its careful, measured movement over the grass toward the eight carefully measured jumps. Margot held her breath in concentration as he guided the horse smoothly, making each stride and jump look effortless. Steven, perched quietly on his mount, looked regal and relaxed. She sighed deeply. He was doing well.

And then, together, they waited while the others rode, and waited while the judge determined which four would return to the ring for the final, more difficult test. The judge would call the numbers in order of her preference at the time. Ah, thought Margot knowingly, number 89—Steven.

Now she listened as the announcer described the test that the four would be required to perform. She shifted slightly, as she felt someone come up closely behind her. Trot the first jump, canter the second, stop. Canter the fifth and sixth jumps at a counter canter.

"What do you think?"

Margot jumped at the ominously familiar voice. "He's doing fine. And it's not over." Her voice hardened. "If you'll excuse me, I'm working now. Very, very hard." She avoided eye contact with him, his father.

"Did you hear, Steven?" She turned back to her student. "Tell me what you have to do. Because your number was called first, so you will be the first rider." She rested her arm across High Flyer's withers.

"Trot the first, canter the second . . ." his voice repeated the judge's instructions, as Margot nodded approvingly.

"What do you think?" Malcolm Forsythe repeated.

"I'm still busy with your son," Margot retorted heatedly without turning. "OK, Steven," she tried to keep her voice even, but a tremor of indignation intervened. She patted his leg again. "Do it."

Then, trying to look impassive, she watched him execute the test perfectly. He'd won, she knew that with certainty. Triumphantly, she turned toward Malcolm. "He did it! He did it!"

Pete took the horse when Steven dismounted, and Margot hugged him with pride. "Great job!"

He held his small silver cup and long blue ribbon for her to admire.

"Now," she whispered, "you have achieved your Medal and McClay and your USET. Now for the Regionals—and the Nationals."

Steven leaned down and kissed her cheek. "Margot, thanks. Thanks a lot," he beamed, and turned to acknowledge the congratulations from passersby.

"Congratulations, Steven," Malcolm stepped forward and extended his hand.

"Thanks, dad. I owe it to Margot." Steven smiled and turned toward High Flyer being led toward the stalls. "And him."

"You seem to owe a lot to Margot," Malcolm commented dryly. "Your mother is in the stands. I saw her with her husband."

"Well, if you both will excuse me, I have other riders to attend to," Margot smiled brightly, when really she wanted to kick Malcolm in the shins. A really intolerable man, even stealing the sun from his son today.

Margot was exhausted when she returned to her farm house. The days of horse shows were long, starting at four in the morning when the grooms would braid the horses and load them on the trailers and exercise them, ending at eight or nine, with relentless classes marching on, one after the other.

Now Margot stretched out on the bed, wrapped only in her terrycloth robe. She wiggled her toes, at last free from the confines of her high black leather boots. She allowed herself the glimmer of Steven's future. She hoped he would succeed beautifully as much for her reputation as for his. And to spite his father. What a loathesome man.

Only the knocking at her door roused her. She peered from the window. Sally stood below, pert and perky in short green shorts and a scrooped-neck T-shirt. "Come on up, Sally. I'm in my room." She stood, waiting, not daring to give the suggestion of a scene on the bed.

"Congratulations. I hear Steven and the others were great today."

"Yes, they were, they learned their lessons well." Margot turned to face the mirror over her bureau, looping her hair high on her head. Her pale cheeks flushed with Sally's presence. "Well? How's Thad, the jumper?"

"Good. I'm making progress. I have a job offer," Sally blurted.

Margot's heart stopped. She felt a terrible tenseness in her body. "And?" she managed, her eyes never leaving Sally's. She waited for the threat.

"I wanted to tell you."

"You wanted to hang this over my head, huh? You wanted to tell me that the job is always open to you so that if you don't become Assistant Trainer in some predetermined number of months, you were going to leave. Is that right?" Margot's voice was hard, almost bitter. "The only thing I know is that you were hired as a groom and no promises have been made about your future. Is that right?"

Sally shifted uncomfortably. "Yeah."

"No deals. Sorry, Sally." Margot dropped her eyes to Sally's breasts, then let them roam down her lean stomach to her thighs and willowly legs. No deals, yet, she added to herself. Her body ached for Sally's touch.

"What do I have to do?" Sally breathed.

"Work. And learn." Margot turned back to the mirror and added black mascara to her eyelashes. She'd felt so tired, yet now she felt so alert and alive with the aphrodisiac of success and Sally. She'd dress and go somewhere.

Still facing the large oval mirror, she dropped her pale green terrycloth robe to the floor and opened her drawer for a beige silk teddy. She glanced in the mirror, noticing Sally's eyes on her. She bent, slipping the teddy, with its high-cut leg openings over her own limber legs, over her waist til it covered her breasts in a well-encased fit. She placed the straps on her shoulders and breathed deeply, her breasts filling the cavities intended to hold them.

Margot looked in the mirror again, her eyes on Sally. Sally had lifted her hands to her own breasts, as if in response to Margot's apparel, and was slowly running her fingers over them, lifting them in round motions. Margot's breath caught, but she stood stock-still, mesmerized by creeping desire.

She watched Sally drop her hand to her shorts and slide her hand up the leg til it bulged at her crotch. Then, again in the mirror, she watched the hypnotic motion of Sally's hand against her genitals. Margot's breath quickened as her senses smelled the turgid lust. Sally's lips parted as her tongue peeped through them, licking them seductively, playing with the corners.

Margot gripped the edge of her bureau, feeling herself begin to writhe. She would explode if she could not take Sally, could not explore each crevice of her perfect body. She swallowed, still gazing, still clutching the edge of the bureau. She heard her own breath in gasps.

Sally stepped forward, placing both hands on the bottom of her T-shirt. She lifted it over her head, exposing her breasts. To Margot, they looked like moist satin. Now Sally placed her hands on the swells of flesh and again began to caress them seductively, lifting and dropping them. Her fingers drifted toward the nipples, lax and waiting, and coaxed them upright.

Margot's pulse hammered, her body electrified by Sally's presence. She scarcely dared breathe as she stared at the woman in the mirror, her own breasts lifting and falling with tension.

Sally wiggled her hips, thrusting them outward,

then backward in alluring little circles, as her fingers massaged her breasts. She dropped her hands and ran them along the contours of her body, swinging her hips to and fro. Her tongue darted outward, licking her lips. She smiled and closed her eyes, even as Margot's stayed glued to the vision before her.

Spasmodically, Margot clutched at the air, longing to grip her in a fierce embrace. Again, Sally stepped closer, only steps away now, so that Margot could breathe in her scent, feel the heat in her body. But if she turned, would she break the spell? Would Sally stop? Would Sally only beckon her further? Her own body swayed rhythmically to Sally's, her own breasts heaved as if she were touching them herself. And then, she gripped the bureau's edge again, feeling as if she would shatter.

Margot bit her lip, trying to stay her own urges. She wanted to fly across the room, take Sally, straddle her and hump her til they came in crashing unison. She wanted the silken feel of Sally against her own body. But she did not move. She merely stared at the image of the woman behind her, tantalizingly massaging her own breasts.

Then, moments later, Sally stopped, as if a sudden phone call had interrupted her, or the doorbell had rung. There was no reason to have stopped, as far as Margot could see. She stared, bewildered, aroused.

"No deals?" Sally whispered, flinging a kiss with her open palm, as she departed. Margot heard her light step on the treads.

Margot stood, hot and heaving on her perch in front of the mirror. Sally had been like an apparition: there, not there, vanishing just as suddenly as she had appeared, leaving only a lingering smell and a kiss wafting in the air.

Margot grinned at herself ruefully in the mirror. She had met her match. Still, though Sally might be intriguing, Margot longed for release. She needed a fast, furious, delightful roll in the hay.

She'd call Corey to let know she was coming. Quickly, she slipped on a blue jean dress over her teddy, scuffed her feet into espadrilles and rushed over to the grooms' quarters. Corey was expecting her.

She walked over to him planting a hard kiss on his mouth, forcing his lips apart. He thrust his tongue toward hers, as she lifted his navy T-shirt toward his shoulders and fumbled for the clasp of his jeans. No point in going through the tedious preliminaries that neither of them needed. Each knew what the other expected and, happily, could easily meet.

Margot trembled with excitement. Deftly, she lifted her loose-fitting denim dress over her head and stood before him in her silken teddy. The bright red on her backside had faded now, so he wouldn't know and she wouldn't have to face the humiliation of telling him the horrors of the night before with Ed.

Corey delicately slipped her underclothing to the floor, and reached for her breasts as Margot undid his pants and pushed them down. She slipped her hand between his thighs, taking his scrotum in her hand, as she took his tool in her mouth. Soon, he gently placed her down on the gray shag carpet and lay next to her, his head next to her mound, her mouth next to his throbbing manhood.

She sighed at the gentleness as his tongue played

among the folds of her flesh and flicked the engorged knob, even as she ran her mouth on his shaft, tickling him with frivolous licks of her tongue. She rolled on top of him so now her breasts dangled above him, resting on his stomach. He drew in his breath sharply as they danced over her hard stomach, and her fingers dipped into his belly. Corey reached his fingers between her legs, playing with the inside of her ass.

Margot gasped with pleasure. She felt swollen with desire, never wanting to leave the comfort of his body, the familiarity of his kind movements. She moved her hips harder against his tongue, and ran her mouth more fervently along his shaft inserting it almost to its full length. Then, mouths pumping against one another, they came in luxurious swells of heat.

"First course," he grinned. He was softer now, but still wet with her passion.

"Main course will be better," Margot nodded, sitting up, as the screen door slammed. Impulsively, she crossed her arms across her chest to shield her breasts from the intruder.

Craig, with his stocky build and shaggy blond hair, wandered in. "Oh, golly." He stopped, wide-eyed and staring. "I didn't know you'd be here, Margot. I—I . . ." he stopped, baffled.

She, too, was baffled. But if she hesitated, unsure, then she would lose the control she had. If she lost it here, then she risked losing it in the barn.

She smiled beguilingly, spreading her arms wide so that her lovely breasts were fully bared. "Might as well join us," she smiled. "Unless you came for something else."

"Um, I didn't exactly come down for this," Craig stumbled. Somehow, his stocky muscles looked awkward here. "I—um—I really came to see if I could borrow—"

"A cup of sugar?" Margot's eye held a glint. Had he really come to borrow something, or just to see them? Or did he think Corey was with someone else worth seeing?

"No, a tape. But," he shrugged. "But—hey, sure, I'll join you," he hesitated, as if he were unsure of what she really wanted. After all, she was still the boss.

Margot giggled. This would be new to the three of them. Just the sort of frolic she'd liked but kept off the farm in the past in case it created jealousies. But now—walking in on them—that delicacy would have to end.

"But you don't look very ready to me," Margot whispered, staring at the soft member before her. "Maybe you should watch Corey and me, just to get into the mood," she cooed, turning back to the tall, blond Corey. She stood up, suddenly hot at the thought of his tongue against her.

"What do you want to do?" she whispered, leaning against the wall next to a photo of Secretariat, the champion race horse. She pressed her hips out, rotating them enticingly, glancing at Corey's manhood, already hardening. He had said nothing. Margot looked at him searchingly. "Do you mind a third?" she whispered.

"No," he replied, leaning forward to nibble at her ear.

Margot pulled her hair out of its clip and let it sweep around the front of her, hiding her breasts and much of her stomach. Corey stepped around, pressing himself against her.

As they pressed and swayed against each other, Corey reached beneath the swathes of hair and felt for her breasts. Margot caught her breath, and then saw Craig stand, ready. He walked to her side, shifting her slightly, so that now he stood behind her. He slipped a hand between her leg while the other reached for a breast. The two men massaged her as she swiveled her hips in joyous excitement.

Corey leaned forward, inserting his member inside her. She arched against him, then felt Craig's hand reach further between her legs til it reached the hilt of Corey's sword not inside Margot. Craig moaned, as his fingers tightened around Corey. Corey pushed harder against Margot as he felt this new, unfamiliar grasp. Margot heard both of their raspy breathing.

She reached behind her thighs, quivering with feverish lust, feeling for Craig. His prick was jammed hard against the outer folds of her ass. She held him, her palm pressing against him as he lunged against her, his cock throbbing wildly.

Margot broke away, falling to the soft carpeting, widening her legs. She held an arm out to Craig to mount her, and another to Corey, to kneel above her. Craig knelt at her head, grabbing her breasts, twitching her nipples to stand like towers. She reached up, urging him to put himself between her lips, as Corey shoved himself between her outer lips.

The tumultuous waves of heat cascaded through them, as she took Craig in her mouth and Corey in her pussy, as these men ran their hands over her stomach, her breasts, her slim waist and long, supple thighs. At last, with cries of delicious agony, the three spilled their passion onto one another.

Breathless, Margot smiled at her grooms. The three lay side by side, heads resting on their crooked elbows, staring at the ceiling.

"Corey, what are those funny white shapes on the ceiling?" To Margot, gazing up from the floor, they looked like circles and crescents and stars.

"Watch." Craig bolted up and turned off the two lamps, plunging the room into near darkness. Suddenly, the white specks gleamed. "They're stars and planets. The cosmos. They light up at night!" he triumphed.

Margot laughed deeply and comfortably and reached for the thin blanket on the couch, burying herself in it. "Who can find me?" she giggled, as she felt the two bodies suddenly scramble on top of her. Wrestling, they took her from the blanket, threw themselves under it and again, fingers fumbling with each other's unknown parts, hands on buttocks and thighs and organs, they again spent themselves.

CHAPTER 8

Margot thought Ed Mason's presence wouldn't make any difference when she mounted his Warmblood, Odds & Sods. But it did. She needed every ounce of discipline to concentrate on the horse.

Those automatic responses to a horse that was not well collected and strung out now failed her. She felt as if she were a new rider, a new trainer. She felt skittish and nervous in front of a teacher. The whip she held in her left hand felt like a cudgel.

Surely, she was embarrassed at her behavior last week. She was embarrassed that she let him beat her, and irritated with herself that she thought of him ceaselessly, in a whorl of excitement she rarely felt.

In the bull pen, just outside the doors of the fading fall day, she heard Sally working her horse, Thad. She'd watched him the other day and was impressed. Sally had nodded confidently, as if she'd known what Margot's reaction would be. Even the other grooms had acknowledged her success with the horse.

At last, Odds & Sods' training was over for the day. Now she could concentrate on herself and her own timid, nervous reactions to Ed with his disarmingly gentle smile and manner.

Margot dismounted, and called for one of the grooms to cool the horse. Hose him down, wrap his legs, she ordered, as she strode out of the ring into the immaculately clean waiting room of brown leather chairs and glass and brass furniture. Her heart hammered, not from the quizzing he would give her about the horse, for she knew that part of her job very well. She didn't think she could play the other part as well.

"What did you think?" she grinned, trying to sound nonchalant.

"Coming along very well. I hear you've had some great successes with your students, especially Steven."

Ed crossed his legs, settling back comfortably in the leather couch, surrounded by sparkling blue and red ribbons and occasional other colors. Silver trophies gleamed from their perches on a three-tier bookshelf.

"Yes, he qualified for the Nationals in everything. In fact, we're off to Harrisburg for the Medal in a few weeks, and the Meadowlands for the National Horse Show in early November." She smiled confidently. Steven's two horses—his hunter and his equitation horse—were serving him well.

"What brings you here? Have you seen Herbert lately?" She asked, nervously making conversation. She wasn't sure what she wanted from him. She wasn't sure what she wanted to avoid either. What she did know was that for days after her experience with him, she had seethed with an inexplicable heat. And now, seeing him again, she felt that same intensity roll within her.

"No, Herbert's been on the islands, every island, it seems," Ed laughed easily, clasping his hands behind his head.

"Free for dinner?" Ed asked, his eyes roaming the one wall where photos of Margot jumping giant fences were lined in neat rows.

She felt a lurch of excitement. "Why. Why, yes," she mustered. The excitement and the fear comingled.

"Why don't you change. I'll wait here, then take you to that steak place just outside of town."

Mutely, stunned with excitement she didn't comprehend, Margot nodded. "I'll be back in a half hour."

She jumped in the jeep she kept parked at the

barn for the times she was in a rush, and raced home as fast as the snub-nosed machine would move. Still, though it grinded and grunted, it was faster than her stride.

A swift shower and a fast change of clothes to a white linen shirt and beige linen pants, a dab of makeup. She sped through her ablutions, not letting herself think of the night.

She had felt sure he would never call her again. For, certainly he could have any girl he wanted to do his bidding. Maybe she'd had the right reaction that night, after all. Maybe her anger and her anguish were what he wanted. She didn't know what she wanted, though. But, now she knew he wanted to be with her. Because if he wanted to talk horses, he could have remained in the lounge and talked horses. He didn't need to do it over a prolonged dinner at Gus' steak house.

Margot returned to Ed, still sitting in the lounge. He stood, eyes appraising her clean, fresh outfit. Then, he led her out of the barn, toward his pristine white Rover.

Margot's eyes darted around the small restaurant, acknowledging acquaintances in the booths and tables. She slid into a seat at the back. She almost felt as if she could see, but not be seen. Ed was silent, but it was a comfortable silence. At last he spoke.

"I think the horse is looking good. I want him in the jumper division."

Margot nodded. "I expected that. He's got a lot of power. I think if we just get his hind end under him a little more, he'll be quite a hit out there." She shook out her red cloth napkin and placed it on her lap, smiling as the waitress came by for their drink order.

The waitress scrutinized Ed, probably the way every other person in America scrutinized the newscaster. Did she recognize him? Did she admire the deep lines that spoke of ruggedness rather than age, the dark eyes as liquid as wells? Did she know his sexual preferences? Did she think this mild-mannered man was the same in the bedroom: acquiescent, subtle, gentle? Margot would only have to bare her welted buttocks to show her.

Yet, even now, as she thought about their night together, she found herself moistening with expectancy. *Had* there been something sexy about it after all?

But she put it out of her mind as his easy banter enchanted her, and their time together passed easily. At last, they stood, heading past the tables before them for the door.

"Margot!" a familiar voice said.

She stopped, peering down at the diner, Steven, alone at a table for two. "Steven, hello." She placed her hand casually on his shoulder, and turned toward Ed. "My prize student, Steven Forsythe. Steven, Ed Mason," she cooed, her hand still resting on his shoulder.

"My favorite teacher," he grinned back, patting her hand. "See you tomorrow?"

"Of course." She squeezed his shoulder, then touseled his hair. She and Ed edged toward the front door.

"Good evening, Margot."

The cold voice stopped her in her tracks. Malcolm. The second setting a the table. Of course. An eighteen-year-old would rarely eat alone. Where had he been? Where did he come from?

"Hello," she said coldly, trying to sidle past him.

"I see you found my son," he added dryly, as he marched past, without further ado.

Margot bit her lip, suddenly worried. That same sense of foreboding that at first had seemed to crush her but then had eased, returned. Just this amorphous sense of doom hanging over her, sometimes hugging her too tightly.

"Malcolm Forsythe," she whispered to Ed, as he opened the screen door for her and they stepped onto the gravel path. "Heard of him? He's supposed to be a big mucky-muck. Steven's father."

"*Heard* of him? I interviewed him. He's a hell of an interesting guy. Very influential in fostering trade with the Soviet block, instrumental in restoring good relations with them."

"I can't imagine him restoring good relations with anyone," she muttered.

"What makes you say that?" Ed walked her around to the passenger side of the Rover.

"He's so bossy."

"He was one of my most impressive interviewees. Enjoyed it. He's smart, considerate, rational. In short, a top-notch man."

Margot smiled dumbly. Did I miss something there? Why does he appear so crude and rude and ruthless? Even when we first met, even before I kicked him out of the ring during Steven's lesson, he seemed on the war path, hell bent to show me that he was in charge. Margot gnawed at her cheek in thought. Was he jealous that Steven was so involved with me? She shrugged. Let it pass. He'll go away. Once he sees Steven's great success, he'll come kowtowing to me.

Silently, she watched Ed slip into his seat and start the ignition. Now what? she wondered with concern. She had a choice. There were two paths that were now diverging. On the one path she'd find her own bed and a safe, predictable haven. On the other, she'd find—she didn't know, but it wouldn't be a solitary night. Did she care? She knew what was in store. Could she bear it? What if he were worse? What if he exacted punishments that she hadn't even been able to fathom these weeks without him? Why would he seek her out again when she so brutally kicked him out? Was it to beat her to a pulp and avenge his ill treatment? Or did he, in fact, like her?

She shrugged again. She so often took charge that the routine bored her from time to time. Suddenly, it felt good to be in the passenger's seat. She'd take the path less traveled.

"I'm not tired yet," she winked coyly. She pulled her long legs in front of her, kicking her sandals off so she could wind her toes in the plush carpeting. She caught Ed's frank glance rove along her body. She wondered if he were thinking of her flaming red behind.

"That's what I like to hear."

Silently they drove through town, where only the lights of the gas station still shown. Finally, he turned up a dirt road not much different from Margot's and stopped in front of a small cabin.

Excitement nipped at her, alternatingly horrifying and electrifying her senses. She swalled boldly as she reached for the door handle. What would follow? Could she survive it after all?

She stepped up a single step onto an overhanging porch, and ran her hands along the round logs that framed the house. Inside, she spied only a living room, kitchen and small dining room, all built around a central fireplace. Upstairs would probably be the bedrooms. Margot stopped, peering about. From behind, Ed took her two arms, pulling them behind her to hold her wrists in one hand.

"Did you come for this? Or more conversation?" He bent her back slightly, breathing into her ear, kissing her neck.

"Why did you want me to come?" Margot's heart hammered, her body began to tingle.

"For this, and only this." He leaned over her tilted face and kissed her straight nose and pale cheeks, never relinquishing her wrists. His other hand came around to fondle her breasts. Brusquely, he tweaked their ends, til she begged him to be gentle. But he did not stop. "I had enough talk," he said hoarsely.

"Please," Margot breathed, squirming, but the nimble fingers plied and tugged at her. Couldn't he at least wait til she saw the upstairs bedrooms? "Please," she moaned. But, then, surprisingly, she felt an enormous heat cascading through her, ready to enwrap her in its folds. She strained forward, trying to break away from him, at least to turn and press her body against his.

Still, he held her as she strained and grunted for release. Through the corner of her eyes she saw his member firmly in his pants, heard his breath coming faster. She relaxed, waiting for him to stop. And just as rapidly as he started, did he stop. He whirled her around to face him.

Roughly, he pulled her pants and shirt from her body, then stood, staring at her heaving breasts and taut stomach.

Suddenly, Ed reached out and ripped her bra and panties to shreds. They dropped limply to the ground.

"What are you doing?" she squealed, horrified. Somehow the rules had changed. He was gruffer, rougher now.

He said nothing, and pushed her forward so she fell against the side of the rough-hewn dining table. "Now this," he whispered, his voice menacing. He lifted a hand and swatted her backside hard. Margot screeched and tried to wiggle away, but his long, strong arm held her. Again and again, he hit her til she knew her buttocks were fiery red. She tossed them from side to side each time he attacked her.

"You saucy thing," he muttered in a choked voice.

His breath came hard, and she felt him fumble with his pants til he could drop his trousers and underwear to the floor. The beating continued, as tears coursed down Margot's face and she howled with the pain and humiliation. The sounds of her yelps echoed throughout the small cabin. Suddenly, he stopped, twisted her around, opened her legs and entered her.

Margot gasped with astonished pleasure as she felt his giant prick inside her. But she could do little more than butt against him. Her body was riddled with pain. He lunged against her, throwing his body at her, til at last, she heard him heave out his passion. Sweat dotted his cheeks and forehead.

"Come," he said huskily, pulling away. He dragged her to a full-length mirror in the bathroom, and turned her head. She gasped at the giant wells on her buttocks. Tenderly, she placed her fingers on them, tracing them over her entire backside as tears streamed down her face. She could only stare in unspeakable disgust at her body.

"Here, try this." Ed handed her a cool wet washcloth.

A different man helped her minister to her wounds. He was so kind, so solicitous. If he cared so much, then why did he do it? She wouldn't see him again. But she scarcely had the strength to yell at him or recoil. All she wanted to do was nurse her seething backside and the pain that seem to shoot throughout her body.

His long, thin member now lay lamely in front of him. What a change, she thought ruefully. He's like a lap dog now.

"Better?" he mumbled into her ear, as his hand took the cloth and gently wiped it over her.

Margot started as a sudden heat flashed through her. How could this be? She'd rarely felt such pain, and yet, astoundingly, she felt wet heat between her legs. She turned, open-mouthed, to stare at Ed as he rubbed her backside in soothing strokes.

"Fuck me," she whispered. "Fuck me anyway you want, but do it now." The urge crashed upon her. She turned toward him and pressed against him, feeling his softening rod at her stomach. She swayed against it til she felt it stiffen. She closed her eyes, envisioning him inside her. He reached for something, and then she felt him take her hands, and quickly, before she could withdraw, she felt him wrap them tightly.

"What?" she blurted, eyes opening rapidly. He had wrapped her wrists behind her in the belt of a white terry cloth robe.

"Oh, no," she cringed. All desire fled just as quickly as it had come. Instead her heart lurched with fear. She couldn't take another beating. "Please," she begged. "Undo me, just undo me. I'll do whatever you want. I hate this. I hate being tied. Ed, please," Margot wailed, pulling away from him in agonized terror. "Please," she begged.

He stood, a slight smile on his lips, his rod growing harder with every wail. "Look, Margot, either you screw or you don't screw. But don't ask for it and then renege. I don't like teases," he said coldly.

"I thought we could do it normally, so it wouldn't hurt," she blurted, as tears rolled down her pale cheeks. She dropped her eyes to his gigantic rod, pulsating with arousal, waiting for her.

"You're gorgeous, just gorgeous," he murmured, running his fingers through her hair.

"Ed, let me go, please," she cried out. "I'll scream. I swear I'll scream." Margot opened her mouth, and just as suddenly, just as surprisingly, the intense longing of before returned with such vigor that she hurled herself forward. "Take me, just take me," she whispered. The heat ravished her, coursing through her as she waited.

"Undo me, Ed, undo me." She struggled against

the rope. "I'll do whatever you want," she repeated, as the heat tore through her. "Fuck me, just do it, now." She no longer knew what she asked him, what she commanded him. All she knew was that the intensity of her longing was unbearable. This man wielded a power over her she hadn't known possible.

He merely shook his head. She writhed toward him, her arms tightly bound behind her. Then suddenly, Ed stepped forward and dropped her to the carpeted floor. Then he mounted her, his body on top of hers. She strained against him as unspeakable pleasure gushed forth.

The minutes drifted to an hour or so. At last, he untied her, spent, exhausted, fulfilled. Tenderly, he rubbed her wrists, admiring their strength and their beauty. She nestled against his long, lean chest, wondering when she'd be able to see him again.

CHAPTER 9

"Margot?" Sally's light voice summoned her on the loudspeaker. "There's a trailer here for High Flyer and Propriety."

Abruptly, Margot stopped Midnight, lightly tapping him with a whip as he came to a walk. A trailer? She thought, puzzled. Why?

She walked her horse to the door of the ring. "Craig, take Midnight, please." She slipped out of the saddle as Craig reached for the horse's bridle. "Why don't you get on him, walk him around?"

Brow furrowed, she ambled toward the burly look-ing man waiting at the office. Several days growth of gray beard bristled at his chin, unkempt hair fell about his shoulders. He loomed over her like a giant gray boulder. Silently, he handed her papers releas-ing Steven Forsythe's two horses.

"I don't understand." Margot's voice hardened as a sudden knot of fear coiled within. So, this was it. That amorphous feeling of foreboding had taken shape. Malcolm was removing his son's two horses. She swallowed, her mouth suddenly dry. What would Steven ride at the horse shows?

"Ma'am, I don't know nothin' about this. I got orders to pick up two horses." The man chewed on gum and waited.

"Where are you taking them?"

"To Forsythe's."

"Forsythe's?" She repeated dumbly. Had Steven given up riding? Had his father hired a private trainer? Was it a ruse so she wouldn't discover the trainer to whom Steven had switched? Margot began trembling. She leaned against the wall to still herself. The humiliation, for everyone knew Steven Forsythe was her student. The ruined reputation. The lost glory. The years of work. The time, the angst. She closed her eyes.

Think, Margot, she commanded herself. Keep the horses. Think, do something. Don't let this happen. Once she would have called Herbert to tell her what clever thing to say. She was tough, she was in charge, but was she smart enough for Malcolm? After all, it was his horses, his money. Was she nasty enough? Unscrupulous enough?

"Ohh," she breathed deeply, trying to quell her nerves. Don't let them take the horses. Keep them at all costs. Why hadn't Steven at least warned her? Or doesn't he know? Should she call him? She wiped her sweat-laden palms on her chaps and again drew in a breath. "Um, OK."

Think, Margot. Your future lies here. You will never get another student of this calibre if you allow this to happen. You will be ridiculed by the industry.

"Look," she spread her hands apart helplessly. "Go get some coffee. I—they're not ready yet."

"Ah, miss," he began.

"OK. There's coffee in the tack room. And donuts. Have a bite."

Margot turned on her heel and entered the office. Sally followed.

"Should I get them ready? What's going on?"

"Not sure yet. No, don't get them ready. And don't show him where their stalls are. I have to make a few calls." Margot picked up the receiver. "It's OK, Sally. I need some privacy now."

Fingers shaking, Margot dialed Herbert's number, even though she knew it was fruitless. No answer, just an answering service. Then she dialed Steven. Again, no answer. Of course, his father would have removed him, absenting him from his plot.

And then, flipping through the rolodex til she came to the proper card, she made the call she knew she had to make. She bit her lip til she felt blood spurt and pressed a knotted fist against her heart as if to calm it.

"Mr. Forsythe, please."

"Who's calling, please?"

"His son's trainer, if you please."

"One moment, please."

The silence thickened as Margot held the receiver to her ear, suddenly unnerved, her thoughts whirling in confusion. She waited for unending minutes, listening to the silence on the other end of the telephone, hearing her heart pounding in her ears. What, in fact, would she say? *Don't take those horses. I have trained them and trained your son. You owe me this.* Would she demand that they remain? Plead? Bargain? *Herbert, where are you? What would* you *say?*

Margot paced back and forth behind the desk. She saw Midnight with Craig on his back walking around the ring, cooling off. She saw Sally lead in Sweet Revenge to long-line him. She saw Pete bring Pennies from Heaven's filly to the bull pen to run around. She heard Corey washing down the mare, Miss Higgins.

Hurry up, Malcolm. I don't have all damn day for this. I have horses to train, a business to run. A stern voice chilled her. This is *your business, Margot.*

"Yes?" His elegant voice burst upon her. It was brisk, hard, to the point.

Margot smiled. *Be cool, be collected. Do not let him hear the fear in your voice.* "Mr. Forsythe? Why is there a carting company at my doorstep with papers for your horses?"

"To remove them, obviously," he said dryly.

She swallowed. "Why?"

"I don't like the way the training is proceeding."

"You *don't?* Why not? Your son has garnered every possible award so far this year, and in just a few weeks he will have the distinct opportunity—"

"I don't like the way his training is going. And I have made other arrangements."

"Mr. Forsythe," Margot wailed, then caught herself. "I think I deserve further explanation."

"I will be more than happy to remunerate you properly. But I want only the best exposure for my son." His elegant voice echoed in her ear.

"You have it." She swallowed. Why was she begging him? Where was her dignity? "You are hurting Steven. He will not be able to ride properly under a new trainer in the few weeks remaining."

"Margot," his voice was suddenly soothing. "Steven wants these awards so much that he will be able to do so. He is prepared to accept a new trainer. Perhaps he would prefer the comfort of you—the nice comfortable fit of an old shoe—but that's not possible. I think a bit of fear facing a new teacher would perk him up, challenge him in these remaining weeks." He was silent.

"Um," Margot began, then stopped. What was there to say? "What do you mean you don't like the way his training is going?"

"It's out of bounds."

"What do you mean?"

"Just that. Margot, I must go. I've got a meeting," he said curtly.

"Could we—you and I—talk about this in person?" Margot felt as if she were grabbing at the wind.

"I don't see what there is to talk about."

"I'd like to explain my teaching methods."

"I'd be interested in that from a purely academic point of view."

"OK, when?" If she hurried, perhaps she could persuade him to send his son back.

"I suppose you'd like to do this soon, in the hopes that you might persuade me to send my son back to you."

"Well, Mr. Forsythe, what *is* the problem? It's not the lessons. What is it?" Margot gripped the receiver, feeling as if she had the strength to break it in half.

"Tomorrow, Margot? I'll stop by at 7:30." He hung up the receiver.

Margot stared at the one in her hand, not yet aware that he had really hung up. He was brutally abrupt. Why had Ed Mason liked him? She couldn't imagine him ever being charming, rational or nice. She kicked at the open desk drawer. Suddenly, a flash of understanding sliced through her. Of course. This wasn't about Steven.

This was about her. Malcolm and her. It was about her rebuffs toward him. And that night, at the restaurant, was the crowning blow: he had seen her with Ed, when he had wanted to be with her himself! Ah-ha! She stamped her foot angrily. And poor Steven gets pummeled about while his father has a hard-on for her. An unrequited hard-on.

Margot laughed bitterly. If she screwed him, she'd get Steven back. Well, Mr. Malcolm Forsythe, you have another think coming. I love my job and I love my business but I won't have you manhandle me this way. The closest thing you'll get to sex with me is a handshake.

She slammed the receiver back in the cradle and stormed out of the office. "Pete, get me Fire Starter. I want to ride him now. And tell that man to get

94

those damn horses out of here."

She took a deep, lingering breath, letting the crevices in her body fill with fresh, determined oxygen. She'd ride that horse til he couldn't buck her anymore, til he was too pooped to gallop another wild, untrainable step. She pulled her chaps down at the ankle, smoothing out any wrinkles at the knee that might give her saddle sores.

I'm glad I've got a stallion like this one, because what I need is a wild, vengeful ride, and at least Fire Starter can give it to me. But somehow I've got to pay Malcolm back.

CHAPTER 10

How long would it really take the hours to pass before it was 7:30? How much longer could the tight string that seemed to wrap her be tightly pulled? Yes, sure she would tell Mr. Big Shot Forsythe how she trained and taught, but there were plenty of other things she wanted to tell him too. Things about fairness and propriety.

She glanced at her watch. She should change. No she shouldn't. She should pretend this was no big deal. She should keep her composure. It was just another sales pitch. People had come to her before, wanting to pull out their horses, and she had always cajoled them into keeping the horses with her. She'd just have to do it again.

But what made her so particularly nervous? What

was it about Malcolm Forsythe that made her composure give way, made her stomach begin to churn? It was different from her reaction to Ed. She churned with fascination for Ed's pranks. With Malcolm, the force of his personality seemed to enrage her.

Malcolm Forsythe had stolen her future. Not her entire future, but her immediate brilliant future, the one that would have been garnered by ushering Steven through the final phases of his horsemanship. Carefully, she wiped her sweat-stung palms on her suede chaps and walked toward the ring.

"Put him away for now, Corey. I think we'll wrap it up for the night." Margot swallowed, hoping that the tears that threatened would be stilled. She wasn't greedy. She didn't feel particularly deserving. She had worked hard, she had nurtured the horses and the boy. Now she just wanted the chance she'd been given. And now, some other trainer would snatch that chance, that victory away.

She walked into the arena, ostensibly to check the kick-boards protecting the bottom of the building from the horses' kicks, but really, to hide away. She made a mental note to have a few repaired. And she wanted a new mirror also on the left hand wall so she could view herself and her horses in all directions. She paced nervously. Would it never be 7:30?

She bit her lip. It wasn't just the horses, she knew. And it wasn't just saying good-bye to Steven, for she had said good-bye to other students also. It was—she hesitated, groping for the word—a mortal embarrassment of having the man pull out his horses. How could she face the malicious gossip that would swirl around her? Malcolm's immaturity galled her, and victimized her.

Margot shook her head as she slowly walked about the arena, inspecting it. In the distance, she heard Craig delivering hay to the horses' stalls and Pete pulling the long hose from stall to stall as he filled their water buckets. Sally would start graining soon. Corey would have barn check tonight at 9:00. Then, tomorrow, the four would rotate their order.

Now she sat opposite Malcolm Forsythe. For a moment, there was only inutterable silence. Not a sound echoed throughout the stable, dark with night, except for the lights illuminating the office. A video cassette recorder sat on a low table between them, aimed at a small television where Margot had just reviewed her work.

The silence stung her. For not a horse coughed or scuffed a hoof along the walls. Margot could only wait. She shifted uneasily in the leather chair.

"Well?" she finally ventured, when he said nothing.

"Impressive. But that is not the issue."

"What is?" she asked defiantly, her chest heaving with unexpected indignation.

"I believe you are inappropriate for my son. My son was to learn riding. I believe, on the basis of the few times I have seen you and from comments he had made, that you have far exceeded the limits of dignity."

"What?" Margot breathed in consternation. "What are you talking about?"

"My son is not to be your sexual toy. Nor are you to be his sexual teacher."

"What?" A shrill bell seemed to peal in her ears.

She stared, dumbstruck, horrified at the accusation. The very thing she had assiduously avoided, she was now being accused of. "I never went near Steven," she whispered, horror hurtling through her. Margot grasped the chair arms, trying to calm herself.

"Margot, I never expected you to admit to this. I never expected much to come from our getting together. But you two exhibit a familiarity that hints at greater intimacy than is appropriate for him." Malcolm's black eyes blazed, his thin nose flared out in anger.

"Then why did you come?" she managed, wiping the perspiration that dotted her forehead.

"To accommodate you. Frankly, my mind is made up." Malcolm stood, shifting his shaggy gray hair off his forehead.

"I—I—" Margot was stupefied, too startled to defend herself. She desperately wanted to curl into a little ball to escape this man. Vaguely, she remembered wanting to escape Ed Mason when he beat her, but Malcolm—he cut to the quick, because he cut to her soul, the precious and private part of her.

And then suddenly as she stared at him, she knew what she had forgotten. Without a doubt, she knew that this discussion had nothing whatsoever to do with Steven. It had only to do with Malcolm and her. He wanted to bed her. He wanted her, and because she had not given herself to him, he was taking his son and her golden future away.

Instantly, her horror turned to fury. How dare he think he could manhandle her this way? Sure, she'd had sex with her customers before. It was the way she kept some who might have moved on. It was the way she rewarded others. And some never got it at all. But no one had ever manhandled her to get it. They waited patiently, hoping for her supple limbs and pliant lips to open for them.

The gall of Malcolm Forsythe. He manhandles international trade tycoons, but he doesn't manhandle me, she thought defiantly.

"I wonder," she began, an unexpected calm flowing through her as she suddenly reconciled the meaning of Malcolm's directive to remove the horses and his son. The absolute knowledge that she understood his desires and was trying to manipulate her strengthened her, steeled her. She boldly met his eyes, as she began again. "I wonder," her voice soft and silky, "if Steven is just a subterfuge."

"For what?" he asked archly.

"Me. Plain old me."

"From what I hear," he said dryly, "I don't need a subterfuge."

"I don't quite understand." But a wedge of annoyance and embarrassment in her stomach told her she did. She understood the insulting implication all too well.

"Lady Cummingham? Walter Metcalf? Rodney St. James?"

Her heart skipped a beat. A hard knot of discomfort. Did they all discuss her at cocktail parties? Just as she counted them off, did they sit around on couches and loveseats and count her off? She took a deep breath, puncuated by several gasps.

Think, think, Margot. She admonished. He's trying to rile you. He's trying to undermine your calm, to bewitch you with his insults. Be stalwart. Don't let him.

She raised her shoulders in a careless shrug. "Then they're the lucky ones, aren't they?"

"Perhaps." His eyes roamed over her body, stopping at her breasts.

Margot lifted her chin defiantly. Yes, Malcolm, look me over all you want, but you shan't have me. I don't care how many horses you have removed from here. She lifted her arms, stretching them backwards so that her breasts protruded like luscious melons.

"I say we don't have much more to discuss, do we, Margot?" Malcolm, unmoved, opened the door, stepping back to let her through first.

As Margot passed by him, she reached for the light switch, casually brushing her breast against his arm. But he didn't respond.

"No, really, we don't," she smiled. "You see, I don't intend to let you screw me. I don't like the way you go about doing it. I don't like your mating dance."

"I see." Malcolm said nothing more as they walked down the wide wooden aisle toward the sliding doors at one end.

"I don't care how horny you get," she persisted, waiting for him to respond. Maybe he'd apologize. Or tell her she had correctly judged him.

"I see," he repeated, still walking, looking straight ahead.

A horse snorted. Another rummaged about his stall for hay, a third lightly knocked the wall. But Margot and Malcolm said nothing. As they emerged from the dark barn, the night was still blacker. Only a few dim lights from the grooms' quarters far at the bottom of the hill broke the thick black about them.

Margot took a deep cleansing breath. It was over. They had had their confrontation. At last she knew what she dealt with. She knew that if she couldn't bear the humiliation of having Steven ride with another trainer, if she couldn't bear the loss, she had only to call Malcolm, and Steven would be returned to her. There was deep comfort in that; elation in the power of her body.

She shifted her feet in the gravelly dirt beneath her. "Good night, Mr. Forsythe."

"Good night, Margot." He started down the hill toward his shiny Mercedes parked near a paddock fence.

Margot headed down the hill in the other direction, toward her home and the grooms' quarters, filled with pleasing confidence.

"Oh, by the way, Margot," she heard him call out genially as he opened his car door. "If you were the last woman on earth, I wouldn't fuck you."

Margot stopped still in her tracks, dumbstruck. *What* did this man want? Maybe he really thought she seduced his son. Maybe that comment was still a smoke screen, that he wanted her very badly indeed. "And I? What do I want?" She wondered aloud.

For no matter how she tried to control herself, she managed to be shaken and buffeted about by him. Anger, remorse, dispair, confusion and excitement raced through her in a parade of successive bursts. And now? How did she feel? Once she cared only about saving Steven. Now she cared about controlling Malcolm. She vowed to show him who, in fact, was running this particular show.

Defiantly, she stood in the darkness watching him pull away in his car. Only the engine's noise, as the car traveled down the dirt drive, determined its position. For the night was so black.

Margot trudged toward the grooms' quarters. This was a night for one of them. If only Malcolm could see. If he could see that she'd screw these guys, but not him. If he could see their ecstacy at her touch, he would be wild with envy.

"Corey," she knocked softly at the door, now closed against the cooling summer nights.

He thrust his head out of the upper window. "Come on up," he called out.

Margot opened the door and met him, naked on the steps. She stopped, her feet on separate treads. With great readiness and no further ado, Corey bent down and kissed her lips deeply, then her throat and chest, dropping to her breasts. His hands roamed over her back and waist and buttocks, as she breathed deeply, drinking in his touch. He leaned down, kissing her hard, as she reached for his member and rolled it between the palms of her hands til it hardened.

"Take me, take me now," she whispered, unbuttoning her shirt so he could find her bare flesh beneath the silky white bra.

Corey dipped his fingers beneath the fabric til he felt the ends of her nipples. Margot pulled down her jeans and her white silk panties, til she stood, half-naked on the stairway. She walked up a couple steps til she stood above him, taller than he.

"Now," she commanded, stepping toward him, inserting his glowing, pulsating member into her waiting cavity. Her hair slipped over her shoulder, dangling down the front of her like a black curtain shielding her body from prying eyes. Margot stepped forward, sliding down upon his upright cock as they stood on the steps. But even as she pushed herself against him and he hammered her, she thought of Malcolm. And when she jammed herself hard against Corey and felt the thrusts within her, she was thinking of Malcolm, wondering how she would ever manage to control him.

At last, she pulled away. She was satisfied in a mechanical sort of way. She'd done the deed but tonight, for some reason, it lost its allure.

And then another horrifying, startling thought crashed upon her. Perhaps she missed Ed. Ed, with his strange passions incited incredible lust within her. The thought of the slaps on her body, the rope at her wrist, made her limp with desire, only moments after she'd finished with Corey. She pressed her legs together as new moisture gathered between them. Could it be that this sort of sex was too tame?

Why was everything in such turmoil?

CHAPTER 11

A strange sort of emptiness pervaded the barn. Everyone knew that Steven Forsythe no longer boarded and rode with Margot. Within hours, Margot learned that he was riding with her key competitor Bill Wainsbert.

She felt a vague sort of embarrassment around her staff, for she knew they felt sorry for her. She lifted her head even higher; being the object of pity had never been on her agenda.

Sally gazed at her across a saddle in the tack room.

"Margot," she finally ventured, "what are you going to do?"

"About what?" she said brightly, covering the gnawing in the pit of her stomach that had awakened her after only a couple hours of sleep, and had never left her.

"Steven. Going to Bill's."

"Well, what do you think I should do?" she smiled gamely. In fact, she didn't quite know. She didn't feel nearly as confident as she hoped she sounded. Another hurried phone call to Herbert had again produced no response. A call to Ed Mason's to see if he knew Herbert's whereabouts had been useless, although they had agreed to have dinner. Dare she ask Ed Mason what to do? No, he was Herbert's friend, he was not her advisor.

Margot smiled again, searching Sally's wide eyes for an answer that she knew she wouldn't find. Last night she had roiled with anger at Malcolm for daring her by removing his son. Last night she would have stomped him to death. But today, the anger had receded, and there was only an emptiness, a sadness at losing this year's dream.

Now she only longed to be comforted, to have warm arms in which to nestle. And there was Sally, as frothy and as impenetrable as ever.

"Go see him," Sally suggested, lifting her brows for emphasis.

"Who?" Margot responded sharply. There was no one left to see.

"Bill, of course."

"Why in the world would I do that?" She asked haughtily. "To ask him not to accept the acclaimed Steven Forsythe as a student. He'd be out of his mind to turn him down. To ask him to do a lousy job teaching him? I couldn't do that to Steven."

"Oh no, Margot. Just to make sure that you are listed as a co-trainer. You don't want to be hustled out of this totally." Sally wiped the saddle cantel with an oiled rag.

Margot looked at Sally, her eyes narrowing in thought. Of course, that must be what she should do. And she should have thought of it herself. She would have thought of it if she hadn't felt so bereft. Instead she said, "Oh, Sally, I really don't give a damn. There will be other students. I have Jenny and Marcy for next year. And, frankly, my reputation is excellent."

"Look, Margot," Sally began. She stretched out a hand toward Margot's. "Reputations need to be reinforced constantly. What you did six months ago is no longer valid if you don't do something today, especially in this world of horses. You can't rest for one second." She looked at Margot searchingly, then dropped her gaze to the saddle she was oiling.

Margot nodded. "Well . . ." she hesitated, ostensibly to mull over Sally's words. But really, she immediately knew she would follow the suggestion. Secretly, she thanked Sally with all her heart, then half-wondered what Sally's motivation was in aiding her. Would Herbert have been as sensible? Was Sally as remarkable as she appeared to be? "Well . . . "

"And the sooner you do it, the better. Don't let Bill think Steven is his for one second. You have to go in and claim your territory. Get Steven to help you."

"No! Absolutely not. I don't want that boy involved in this. He should not have to bear the tribulations of a weird father." Margot heaved a sigh. For that was the only thing she really knew.

Margot clasped her free hand on top of Sally's, squeezing it gently. She didn't like to admit weakness to the girl. Sally shifted her weight slightly, as if the contact affected her.

"Margot, by the way, how do you think my training on my horse is going?"

Margot jerked upright. Ah, an ulterior motive. That's why I got the advice. She expects something in return. Now is the time she'll ask to be an assistant trainer again.

Sally gracefully pulled away from Margot and slid to the floor, against a wood-panelled wall. "Tell me what you think," she said softly, the oily cloth laying on the ground next to her.

"I think he's bending very nicely now. I'd like to see a bit more flex in the head." Margot swallowed uncomfortably. She didn't want to talk horses just then. She wanted to sit next to Sally and hold her for succor.

With effort, Margot raised her eyes to Sally's, and continued as if nothing were happening. "I'd like to see a bit more collection in his hind end."

"And how would you suggest I do these things?" Sally asked, toying with the oiled rag.

Margot swallowed, her irritation palpable. Of course she had to answer these questions, but each time she did she knew she was inextricably binding herself to Sally even further. "I'd long-line him some more, work him from the ground."

"Oh, thanks," Sally gushed, standing. "I thought I needed to do that, but I wasn't sure." She beamed with joy.

If you're so sure of what you need to do, then why ask? Margot thought glumly. But suddenly she was tired, very tired. Tired of the sparring and the cravings.

She felt beleaguered on all sides. Sally. Malcolm. Ed. She needed to enfold in kisses and caresses Sally's soft suppleness, and she needed to pummel to a pulp Malcolm's hard mean body.

She shook her head. A terrifying and immediate urge to be rid of Sally overwhelmed her. She pulled herself upright.

"Thanks for the advice, Sally," Margot said coldly. "I'll think about it." She then turned on her heel and headed for the jeep.

She stopped, her hand gripping the chrome handle, hot from the sun. Oh, hell. So much to think about. So much to be plagued by. She imagined vultures plucking at her eyes and her innards, one by one, til there was nothing left.

OK, Margot. Get hold of yourself. OK. She sighed deeply and tugged at the door. Think about Malcolm first. Sally is your afterwork dilemma. "OK," she muttered aloud. "OK. I'm under control now." She turned the key in the ignition. "And right now I'm going to talk to Bill." Sally was right. She couldn't just take Malcolm's actions passively. Somehow she had to fight back.

Sally. She was some smart cookie. Sally gave just the sort of advice Margot would have given someone. It was wily. It was cogent. There was a reason Margot was so attracted to her. And it wasn't just that red-haired, freckled body.

She backed away from the fence and spun the jeep around, heading out the dirt road. Bill, she hummed. He wouldn't forsake her; she hoped. They'd always had a friendly rivalry, but they had never purposely undermined each other; they had too much respect for the other's abilities. They'd learned about horses together and taught together, and then became friendly competitors. They'd even do favors for each other: lend a bit or a girth, borrow a groom at a show.

But, despite these favors, Margot wasn't sure how far his good will toward her *really* extended. Would it extend as far as Steven Forsythe?

Margot wasn't quite sure what she was going to accomplish by seeing him. Certainly she couldn't persuade him to drop Steven as a student. At best she could persuade him to enter both his name and hers as his trainers.

Margot waved at Bill as she drove the jeep over a bumpy grassy road edged with two-by-fours toward the barn.

"I was expecting you," Bill grinned at Margot in the jeep. The crooked smile flashed in his still tan, but weathered face, the crows feet and smile lines well etched above his square jaw. Margot looked up to his 6′ frame, at the brilliant blue eyes and blond hair.

"I lost my best student. Did you think I was just going to sit around. I've come to negotiate," she called jauntily from the window. Then she hopped out and planted an engaging kiss on his lips. "Let's talk turkey. I don't want that bastard Malcolm Forysthe to exclude me on the credits as a trainer."

"Geez, I don't know. He's pretty riled up. Says you seduced his son."

Margot stepped back and peered up at Bill, shading her eyes from the sun's glare. "You believe that? You know my rules. Anyone, *besides* my students, is fair game."

"I don't really believe it. What do you think he's doin'? He must be pretty riled up to take his son away. He's riskin' everything, cause that boy won't ride as well for me, especially if he doesn't really want to be here. I think the old man misjudged you, thought you were seducin' the boy when you weren't."

"I think he wants to get in my pants," she grinned. "Like you." Margot reached out, hooking her thumb in Bill's leather belt. "Can you help me?"

She'd never been so bold with him before. Usually, there were days of give and take, sly dancing around each other, til one relinguished something and the other relinguished something else. But now there was no time. And she had nothing to offer.

"Geez, Margot, I can try. We're set for Harrisburg in a few weeks. I've been workin' with the kid. He's good, real good. But he's rattled. He's lost some of what I saw he had at the Regionals. And I don't know if he can get it back with me. He likes you. He feels lost with me."

"So what are you doing for him?" Margot stood next to Bill and put her arm around his waist. It felt good. She remembered fondly their times together.

"Spendin' time, a lot of time, so he gets to know me, and feels comfortable with me. He's here now, in the barn."

"Should I see him?"

"Sure, tell him you support him, at least."

"OK, but if I tell him that I support this move and that I know he can be as great a rider with you as he was with me, I help you. A feather in your cap. What goes in mine?"

So she did have something to offer, after all, she congratulated herself. Bill didn't think Steven could perform. Bill did need her help.

"I'll ask the old man to include your name as co-trainer."

"Not good enough."

"I'll insist upon it tonight when he comes by."

"Not good enough."

"I'll have it in writin', signed," Bill grinned. "Still a tough negotiator, Margot."

"Then let's celebrate after we see Steven." She winked.

Bill answered her wink with a nod. They'd always sidestepped each other verbally, but never sexually. There was no subtlety there.

Margot had done her best, given Steven her best encouragement even though she knew it would do no good. He had lost a spark, gained a sadness. She had patted his shoulder, barely able to refrain from attacking his father. But now she shrugged it away, as she clambered up the wide wooden staircase to Bill's apartment above the barn.

"So we have a deal?" she asked lightly, as he poured her some hot coffee.

"Yup. You did your best. But you sure you want to be associated with him in case he doesn't carry the day?" Bill sat down at the butcher block table, swinging both his legs over the arm of a Breuer chair.

"Yes, he'll do fine enough. If you tell Steven that we're both listed as trainers, that might give him some impetus. What do you think?"

Margot sipped her coffee. "Good to be back, here, Bill. Haven't chatted in months. What's going on?" She eyed his little apartment, scattered about with horse magazines and video tapes, an unmade queen-size bed and an enormous closet covering the back half of the bedroom. Several layers of blue jeans were tossed over the back of a straight back chair that seemed to serve as a giant suction cup for clothing.

"Not much. Seein' some girls. No one special."

"Me neither," she winced, as she thought of Ed Mason who, even in his absence, enticed her. Did Sally count? Even if she bedded her, would she count as someone Margot saw?

Margot stood, ambling toward the closet. "Got the same old good stuff?" She pulled at the folding doors and rummaged in the back of the closet. "Ah," she announced, pulling out a black leather garter belt and small black leather vest that would scarcely cover her breasts. She walked inside the large closet, hiding herself from Bill.

Quickly, she stripped off her clothes, letting her

jeans and panties, T-shirt and bra drop to the ground, knowing Bill would still be sipping his coffee placidly. She knew he heard her, knew what she was doing.

"I'm taking off my clothes now, Bill," she said softly. "And now I'm slipping the small black vest over my arms, settling it down on my shoulders, placing it across my tits." She heard him rustle.

Margot bent over, lifting the leather garter belt with its silver rings hanging from it like fringe. She fastened it around her waist, letting the rings dangle from the leather at her hips. "Now I'm fastening the garter belt around my waist. Ah, I've just clipped it on," her voice was soft, beguiling.

She rummaged around a clear plastic box for the old fishnet stockings she used to wear. "Ohh," she cooed, "the beautiful stockings. I'm slipping my right toe into one, pulling it over my foot, over my ankle, up my calf, over my knee, onto my thigh. I've just closed it. Now I'm doing the other," she continued purring.

The chair that Bill sat on scraped along the floor. She felt for the high-heeled patent shoes she'd seen in the back corner, and slipped her feet into them. Then, shrugging, she opened the closet door and stood, framed by it, facing Bill.

He moved to stand, but fell back onto the seat again, staring avidly. Margot shrugged, letting the vest fall open slightly, exposing the tips of her breasts like high beams on an Alpha Romeo.

"Now, Bill," she let her breath roll out, "I'm letting my hair out." Margot pulled at the clasp, letting the sheath of shiny black hair enfold her.

His mouth was open, his eyes agape. His hand gripped his coffee mug tightly, but even so, she could see he trembled. She walked over to Bill, still sitting at the chair. But one look at his crotch told her he'd not been unaffected. She smiled in merriment as she spied the enormous protrusion within his pants. Ah, that was what she remembered about him: the clothes, and the thick length of him.

Margot stood a few feet from him, swaying her hips, as her fingers ran about her body, over her thighs, her hips, her waist, her breasts. Bill's mouth opened, his tongue dropped out, his hand found his crotch. He watched her wiggle her hips, sway her tits in alluring circles.

Deftly, Margot stepped forward to unzip his pants and unfasten the button on top. With difficulty, she freed his hard member til it stood upright, at attention. She stepped back to her former position just a few feet from him.

"It's so good to see you," she breathed, her tongue sliding over her lips, her hips pulsating forward and back. She turned and bent down, splaying the folds of her ass, then ran her hands up her legs, over the curves of her waist to her breasts. When she turned around, Bill's eyes were glowing, his hand feverishly working on his rod.

"Ohh, there's no need for that," she breathed, bending over him. Her breath glanced off the tip. She removed his hand, placing it on her breast. Then she wound a thick ribbon of hair about his shaft, pulling til she saw the veins pulsate within.

She leaned forward, teasingly touching his chest with her barely covered breasts. She looked up, her tongue licking at her lips til, at last, Bill leaned forward, and kissed her.

Their tongues played together, as his fingers ran over her breasts. Margot drew her breath in swiftly at his touch. His fingers touched her nipples, kneading them til her body throbbed. Then, slowly, she unwound the ribbon of hair that bedecked his shaft. Round and round, she pulled the plaits of hair from him. He groaned and reached for her, but she sidestepped him, throwing her hair behind her shoulders.

"Lie down," she whispered, easing him to the ground. Adroitly, she placed his clothes on the rag rug beneath them, and sat on his hips, her legs straddling him. She flipped her hair forward, running long black strands over him, as if she were sweeping him away. He rocked to and fro, groaning with pleasure.

Then he reached out, felt for her hot center beneath the contours of the black leather garter belt and black fishnet stockings. Margot gasped at his touch, lurging forward as pleasure radiated through her. His tongue made a path from the tips of her breasts, down her navel, across her hips and to her inner thighs.

Margot spread her legs further, pushing his fingers inside her still further. His hands seared her as they felt her breasts, kneaded her buttocks and toyed with her hungry cavity. At last, thinking she would burst, she slid down, sliding herself upon Bill's waiting shaft. Her hair spread out in front of her, covering his hard stomach, as she grabbed at him in a sudden wild fever til they were spent.

Giggling, Margot fell forward, kissing his hard chest. "I love dress-up clothes. I love fucking you, Bill." It was comfortable, like an old shoe. She felt as if a bolt had gone through her. Malcolm had used that word in describing her: an old shoe. Bill was comfortable. Ed was the unknown.

Margot stood and stretched. "Guess I better go back. Got some things to do.

"OK, then," she called out gaily as she began to back the jeep. "We have a deal."

"Got a deal, Margot," Bill answered, a friendly lopsided grin covering his face. "Try my best."

"Not good enough, sport," she giggled, feeling confident. He'd come through. But would Steven?

CHAPTER 12

"Stop, I beg you, stop!" Margot screeched, as her body hurtled across Ed Mason's bed. Tears coursed down the front of her blotched face. "Stop. No more," she panted, pulling at the laundry line that bound her wrists to the wooden headboard of his double bed.

But, still he raised his hand with the belt and brought it down on her buttocks. Vaguely, through her own labored breathing, laced with pain, she heard his panting. She twisted as the pain of the switch sliced through her. How long had he been doing this? How long had she been his prisoner, beneath his strong hand, his piercing eyes, his excited but hushed tones?

Perhaps if she made no noise, if she simply gritted her teeth and bore it silently, he would stop. She buried her face in the pillow to muffle the screams she desperately wanted to release. The pillow was wet with her tears. The belt slammed into her again. But she merely gritted her teeth in anguish.

"Say something," Ed said, bending over her, his hard cock brushing against her back. "How much do you hate it? Say it." His voice was intense, laced with malice. "Say it." Again, he brought his full force upon her. Margot writhed and wailed. As she turned, she saw her reflection in the mirror covering nearly all the wall.

She saw her pert buttocks and slim waist flailing about with the torture, saw her breasts heave with the exertion. And saw the glowing pink that striped the cheeks of her backside. Horrified, yet hypnotized, she couldn't remove her eyes from the sight.

Ed stood above her, watching her in the mirror, a smile of satisfied glee pasted to his face. His cock stood huge like a club to be wielded, pulsating with its own activity. "What do you think?" He breathed. He slapped her buttocks with the flat of his hand.

The sting shot through Margot. She howled, but somehow, fascinated, watched herself in the mirror. And suddenly, bizarrely, a flash of heat swelled through her. The tingling grabbed her in her cunt, flooded through her limbs, cascading through her like a waterfall washing over her. Her senses reeled with a delicious flood of ecstasy beneath his hands.

"Oh, God, Ed, do it, do it," she moaned, pulling her wrists tightly against the rope so it cut into her.

"Again, oh, please," she moaned. Now it was a moan of both desire and pain as he brought the strap down on her again. She arched her back. The reflection in the mirror caught her straining and twisting, her black hair wreathed about her body like a dark shroud.

Margot lurched upward and back, trying desperately not to climax amid the feverish passion and the pain. An intense desire, unlike any she had ever felt, ripped through her, threatening to tear her apart. She gasped, longing for his thick cock inside her, praying for release.

"Take me," she pleaded. "Do it, do it now," she begged, her voice rising with her crushing need for satisfaction.

He lashed at her again. She saw herself writhe with pain and felt that surging flame inside.

"Take me," she gasped, rolling from side to side, her legs flapping with the bonds of frustration.

He said nothing. Only his heavy breathing broke from him like a sinister mad magician. Margot recoiled from the stings of the switch, even as giant rolls of intense heat pummeled her.

Abruptly, Ed was upon her, falling upon her back, lifting her slightly and entering her yearning cavity. His hands clamped around her breasts, and he rode her, as they strained against one another in a heady stream of lust.

At last, he rolled off, next to her on the crumpled gray sheets and maroon comforter, his breathing still heavy, his eyes closed. Now, his member receded, the club-wielding giant just a shadow of his former self. Margot fell forward, spent. She scarcely felt the rope cut into her wrist. And only when he laid a light hand on the welts on her bottom did she wince.

"Oh, God, do you ever think I'll be able to mount a horse today?" she wondered. She also wondered if she would ever have the energy to do so. She was exhausted, spent, wildly joyous.

"Sure," Ed reached up and unfastened her wrists. He rubbed the gouges softly between his palms. "If you sit up very straight on your cheekbones. I left them alone."

"You mean you had a method?" Margot was surprised.

"Of course, I didn't want to hurt you." Tenderly, he ran his fingers across the streaks.

"Well, you did."

"Ah, Margot, don't say that. It makes me feel bad."

"Do you always do this?" She sat up facing him, grimacing as a streak of pain flashed through.

"I like it. And so do you." He stood and offered her his hand. "Let's take a shower and talk about it later."

Gently, as the water pelted her body rinsing the searing pain, Margot felt herself begin to heal. But the memory enticed her. Even as she stood under the water, feeling its soft touch and remembering the lashes, she felt herself moisten once again. She reached out, taking his member in her hands, softly pulling it til it began to harden within her grasp. She thought she'd burst from waiting.

"Take me," she whispered. "Do it." She opened her mouth to lap up the shower water and opened her legs, hoisting herself around his hips. Then she guided him inside under the gentle stream, and pushed herself hard against him til the last little drops were spent.

Even the early morning couldn't mask the gray day, couldn't pretend that the sun would soon rise on a glistening fall day. She fumbled for the phone by her bed, and froze as she heard Bill's voice.

For she knew, without his saying so, that Steven had not made the cut. He'd gone to Harrisburg to compete against one hundred other junior riders. He'd need to make the first cut to the top twenty five. Then he'd need to make the second cut to the top ten. And then, be number one. But this call was too early. It meant he had failed. For had he made it, Bill and he would have been preparing for the second stage of the ride.

"He didn't do it, did he?" Margot mumbled, sitting up.

"Nah, he was out of the ball park. We been here two weeks. I wanted to shake him up by throwing him in with the competition, try to have him forget you. Didn't work. He just didn't have it for me."

Margot nodded, rubbing her buttocks, still sore with the exertions of the other day. "I know. His father screwed him."

"I'm going to recommend that he not go to the National Horse Show in November. I don't think he can pull it together."

"I oughta kill his father. Or he oughta." Margot stretched. She felt strangely aloof from it all. At last. She might as well start her day. She had a number of horses to work, and she had a couple people coming to buy as many as she could sell. "When are you

119

coming back? Let's get a strategy together."

"Leavin' in a couple hours. Steven's down in the dumps, too."

"I could give Steven a pep talk."

"He doesn't need a pep talk. He needs a trainer." Bill hung up.

Margot stared at the phone, seething. "That bastard father. He ruined his kid's life all because he wanted to get in my pants. He thought he was ruining my life. But I have other kids coming along. I didn't *really* need Steven, not like he needed me."

She stepped into the shower, washed herself, and then donned her regular attire of jeans and a long flannel shirt. These days the mornings were cold, the evenings were cold. There were just a remembrance of tepid summer days around noon.

"No, he's a creep," she said aloud. "And someone should tell him." She bit her lip with determination, and then strode down to the office in the barn. Quickly, she flipped through the rolodex til she found his card. She slammed the door shut with an outstretched leg. She didn't need her grooms overhearing this.

"Malcolm Forsythe, please." Her voice quavered.

The interminable minutes passed until a voice blithely asked who was calling. Then, more interminable minutes passed with the thick silence of a disapproving aunt. It was as if the phone knew she were an unwelcome caller.

"Yes, Margot?" Malcolm's voice was airy, polite, inquisitive.

"You screwed your son."

"Apparently," he retorted dryly.

She stared at the receiver, at a loss for words. He was so unresponsive. What was she to say? "You screwed him," she repeatedly for want of anything else to say.

"I think we should talk, Margot." He remained friendly, but she detected a hint of annoyance. She could imagine him rubbing his gray hair back with his hand, glancing at his watch with annoyance, perhaps rolling his eyes toward a colleague. "What do you say if I come by tomorrow at seven. I'll pick you up."

She pulled back, resenting his assumption that she was free for him. "I'm busy," she answered politely. "We'll have to do it another night."

"I have a rather tight schedule, Margot." His voice was suddenly granite-hard. "Why don't you make yourself free."

She heard the click of the phone as he hung up.

"Why don't you make yourself free?" she mimicked, aloud. "Do my bidding, dear. Well, fuck you." She stomped her foot. "You got the wrong person, here, Mr. Smartypants. You think you control the world and your son and your horses. But you won't control me."

At 7:00, Margot was watching blue movies with Bill, back from the horse show in Pennsylvania. They sat side by side on the floor, leaning against his gray tweed couch, a bowl of popcorn between them, gazing at short films of people having sex, joyless, mechanical sex. Margot wore only her one-piece black lacy teddy; he wore just his white shorts with garish blue dots.

Bill's hand lay at the entrance to Margot's sex, his

121

fingers diddling with the folds of flesh, as her fingers rested easily on his hardening prick. Carefully, casually they fondled one another, feeling the heat between them spreading as they watched the actors in the color film lick and prod one another.

Margot was damp with expectation as he gently fingered her. His fingers slipped beneath her, trailing to her ass. She began to tighten and release her pelvis, feeling that familiar, welcome tingle. She raised her own fingers to Bill's navel and heard him suck in his breath. She dropped them again to his shaft, beneath his shorts.

They never looked at each other, merely rubbing and watching the movie. Margot gripped his rod harder as she felt her own heat spread, as the man in the movie bent to lick the woman's vagina. She felt Bill tremble within her grasp, as his fingers worked her more forcefully. Spasmodically, she squeezed the muscles in her pelvis and thighs, pushing against his fingers.

Bill reached within the bodice of the teddy, feeling for her nipples, already taut with desire. He tweaked them. Margot rested her head against the seat and closed her eyes.

"You don't like the movie," he whispered, fingering her.

"I like this better."

"If you watch the movie, you'll like this better," he retorted, running his hand over her soft inner thighs.

She nodded, focusing on the couple before her, listening to the projector whirling.

Bill stopped, resting his hands lightly on his knees. But Margot continued to rub him. "What are you going to do about Steven?"

"Tell his father he's cruel, see if that does any good." She glanced at him, then returned her eyes to the screen.

Bill leaned over, kissing her cheeks, chin and eyes, as he rubbed her breasts.

Now, the woman had climbed atop the man, licking his cock. He reached for her legs, swinging her about, to return the gesture.

"That gives me a good idea," Margot mumbled. She scooted her body around and bent over Bill, taking his engorged member from his shorts. She slid around, so he could reach her.

"Can you see?" he mumbled, as he kissed her mound.

"Yup," she answered back, her lips running up and down his shaft, her fingers fondling the skin around it.

And as the couple on the screen lapped at each other til they came, so did Margot and Bill, never taking their eyes off the screen.

Margot fell forward, wiping the remnants of Bill from her mouth. She toyed with the hairs on his thighs, as he flexed and fondled her toes. "I love going to the movies," she giggled. "Where's the popcorn?"

"Under you." He laughed. "Check it out."

Margot twisted to see. The bowl had tipped. The popcorn kernels had rolled under the couch or plastered themselves to her legs and backside. "Guess we have a lot of cleaning to do, Bill," she giggled, picking one up and placing it on the top of his flagging rod. She ate it off its perch.

Finally, she stood. "I probably need to go. What time is it?" She had to make sure it was well after 7:00. She had no intention of seeing Malcolm. He would have left after a half hour for he was not one to wait around. She shrugged and tossed her head, as she slipped on her clothes. She'd show him that she, for one, could not be bought.

Now she turned to face Bill. "Tell Steven to ride his best. He can do it."

"Margot, he can't do it. He can't git used to me in just a couple weeks. And he doesn't want to git used to me. *He* wasn't tired of you. Did you find out what really happened?"

Margot nodded. "I'm sure he just wanted to get in my pants."

"Well, maybe you should let him."

"That bastard?"

"You've fucked worse, honey."

"That was to get something, it wasn't to get *back* something that belonged to me." She shook her head. "Nah, someone should teach him a lesson."

"Let someone else do it. Just get your boy back. You're hurtin' him."

Margot lifted her shoulders helplessly. "So is his father. Why should I be passively selfless to assuage that man's ego? Look, I like Steven a lot, but if it gets around that I screwed his dad so I wouldn't lose him as my student, my reputation is not going to be enhanced." Margot readjusted her teddy.

"S'pose you're right." Bill stood, looking for his jeans. "Anyway, this situation gives me the rare opportunity to git together with you again."

"Isn't that worth *something?*" She teased.

CHAPTER 13

"I don't like to be kept waiting."

Margot jerked to a halt. The voice penetrated the darkness, as if it surrounded her on all sides. "Yes?" Her voice quavered.

"I told you I would be here at 7:00."

"*I* told you I was busy," she retorted, standing next to the white rail fence by the dirt driveway. She squinted in the blackness, turning her head from side to side, trying to decipher him. But the darkness masked him.

"I told you I wanted to talk, and that I had limited time."

"I should think you'd create more time for your son." Margot took a step forward. If only she could get to the front porch of her farmhouse. There the outside lights, on either side of her door would protect her. At least she could see her inquisitor.

"If you cared about him, as you profess to, I should think you'd be available." The voice followed her, just paces behind.

"What *is* it that you want?" Margot blurted crossly. She was no longer afraid, just irritated that he tried to frighten her.

"I want to talk about my son." He followed her up the steps.

With relief, Margot turned to face Malcolm, no longer an apparition in the night. He towered before her, eyes smoldering with anger. His broad shoulders blocked her passage into her safe house.

"Talk," she commanded.

"May I come in? It's a bit nippy." His voice softened. It was almost congenial.

"All right," she said reluctantly, pulling the screen and the wooden door open. Where had he waited for her these past two hours while she screwed Bill?

She turned on the lamps in the living room and sank into the soft wing chair next to the fireplace. He sat opposite her in a low tub chair. A small table set the barrier between them.

Malcolm cleared his throat. Was he nervous? Margot thought maliciously.

"Steven did not perform very well at the last horse show."

"Is that so?" she responded dryly.

"Why is that?"

"He missed me," she chirped.

"I didn't ask for glibness."

"I didn't give you glibness. I told you the simple truth. You yanked him from me. These are delicate relationships between student and trainer and you made sure to wreck it." Margot kicked off her dark brown topsiders and pressed her bare toes into the multi-colored rag rug beneath her feet.

"Should I reconsider? I don't usually like to reconsider."

"Shows weakness, does it?" she asked bitterly. For he had hurt her when he removed his son from her care.

"I reconsider only if I see renewed potential in a failed project."

"Look, Mr. Forsythe," Margot jumped up and stood before him, hands on her hips, eyes blazing. "Nothing was failed. it was just your imagination. He was riding beautifully. You were just angry that you couldn't boss me around. You were angry that you couldn't get in my pants. *That's* the truth."

"*That* is not the truth. I think you were in my *son's* pants."

"I don't believe you," she said simply, turning away. She walked to the side window and stared out, as if she could see something. In truth, on that particular night, she saw only her own reflection encircled in the lamplight.

"I am prepared to return my son and his horses to you."

Margot held her breath, waiting for the rest. She knew that Malcolm, like Sally, gave nothing for free. "And?"

"And I'm prepared to do so tomorrow."

Margot wheeled around, eyes wide with unexpected delight. "What do you want from me?"

"I want you to make him win again. Put the fire back in his belly." Malcolm looked up at her. His voice was laden with sincerity and emotion. He had become the father of a beloved son. He was no longer the swaggering braggart. "Is it too late?"

She shrugged. "I suppose the horses are still in good working order under Bill's tutelage. The question is your son." Margot stared at Malcolm. "I think you did a despicable, rotten thing to him. I will never believe that you honestly thought I was seducing him. But I think Steven's a terrific rider and a terrific kid. And I'll work very hard to restore everything."

Margot turned toward the fireplace, picking up a long match lying on top of the mantle. She scraped at the end with her fingernail, waiting for Malcolm to stand and leave.

When she heard no movement, she turned back and stuck out her hand. "Please come by in the morning to sign some papers," she said formally. "And now I'd like to call it a night." She kept her voice even, but she felt like dancing with joy. She wanted to whoop and cry out. Steven was back, her beloved Steven, her future had returned! And she had beaten Malcolm, to boot!

"Fine," he said preemptorily, his feet scraping along the oak floor as he stood.

Margot watched him walk across the front porch, across the grass and slip into some little foreign car parked on the grass, not on the driveway.

"Figures," she muttered, but not unkindly. For Steven was back.

The stalls were readied, loaded with fresh water, fresh hay and fresh bedding, when the two horses arrived the next morning. Steven walked in later in the day, outfitted in beige breeches, high black riding boots, his velvet huntcap and a wool sweater.

"Ready to ride?" Margot smiled, as if nothing in the world had happened. "You know, sometimes after a hiatus, people are even better than before. Maybe this little break was helpful."

"I don't know, but it made me miserable. No matter what I said to my dad, it didn't matter. What made him change his mind?" Steven wondered as Sally tacked up High Flyer.

"You," Margot answered directly.

"How?"

"Your awful performance. He saw he couldn't just

boot you around."

Steven nodded. "I told him you weren't after me."

Margot saw Sally glance quickly at her, but return her eyes to the bridle she was tightening. "He'll believe what he wants." She shrugged. No point telling him that his dad wanted to bed her. "Come on, let's see what Bill taught you."

Smiling with happy anticipation, Margot followed Steven and his horse into the arena, an air of contentment enveloping her.

She felt a peace that she hadn't felt in many, many weeks. For Steven would be just fine.

Now the only question was Sally. Where in the picture would Sally fit?

CHAPTER 14

"What do you think now?" Sally demanded from her perch atop her horse.

Margot stood in the center of the ring watching Sally's grace as she guided Thad over foot-high vertical jumps, and brought him to an easy stop.

"Great. He's looking good." She headed for the door, prepared to ride.

"Uh, Margot," Sally walked her horse closer, patting him on the withers. "When can I be assistant trainer?"

"Why do you want to be one?" Margot tried to remain calm even as she asked this question. She'd known it was coming. She'd known Sally would be back with the persistence she'd shown in training horses. But, faced with it, Margot still didn't know precisely how to handle it, except to deny her the opportunity.

To let her be a trainer would undermine the other grooms, would open her up to derision from other trainers who never handed out the title after so little time. To let her be a training would mean she'd have to spend the rest of her days looking over her shoulder, wondering if she were being fragged by her employee.

"I want to be a trainer so I can start to build my reputation," she answered simply.

Margot pulled back, eyeing Sally, still walking about the ring. She'd thrown a wool cooler over Thad's rump, to keep him warm and absorb some of his sweat.

"And then leave here?" Margot pressed.

"No, not for a while. I told you that. You have a lot to teach me."

Did she wink, Margot wondered, almost hypnotized by Sally's blazing eyes.

"How long? Two months? Six months? Look, Sally, you're the best groom I've had, you're a helluva terrific trainer. But there's too much at stake."

"Here's a deal. If you make me a trainer, I'll stay three years. If you don't, I'll stay about six months longer." Sally pulled the cooler over her thighs so it didn't drag on the ground.

Margot stared in wonder at Sally's audacity. She was horrified, but at the same time fascinated. Margot herself had not been shy, but she'd never really asked for her promotions outright. She'd fucked her

130

way there. She'd blown her way there. She'd arched, lurched and rammed her way there. Sally just asked outright; and she didn't offer anything in return.

"I don't think so, Sally. It's too soon. You'd have nothing to strive for." She tried to keep her voice calm and controlled. But she felt rising anger and a sort of panic. What if Sally left? Silly, she admonished herself. Other grooms have left. But there have been no others like Sally, she replied inwardly.

Perhaps that was why Herbert purchased this farm for me; he was afraid I'd leave. He was afraid that after I said I'd love my own place and after I'd sucked him off in front of that wonderful waterfall, that I'd hop up and bid him adieu forever. He was afraid, and he gave me what I wanted.

Icily, Margot stared at Sally. She knows. She knows I want her body. She knows I've watched her in the shower, watched her with Pete. She knows I'm afraid to lose her, that she'll never have another opportunity like this again with any other trainer. No other trainer will crave her as I have. So she thinks I'll cave in.

Margot lifted her head with defiance. "Not good enough," she smiled.

"I get the title, but I continue to muck the stalls, do the tack," Sally ventured.

"No dice. There's not enough work for two full-time trainers."

"I'm not asking for any other horses. I'll keep the ones I have, do the work I currently do, and have a better title."

"Then the title becomes meaningless," Margot retorted, suddenly tired of the strain.

She was always negotiating. First with Malcolm, then will Bill, now Sally. Wasn't there just a way to say no, and have it stick? Couldn't she just easily get her own way?

"Then I'll leave in a few months," Sally reiterated.

"Well," Margot hesitated, as if she were thinking, but really she knew what she was going to say. "Give me a couple weeks to think about it."

"You don't need a couple weeks." Sally hopped off the horse, then lifted a stirrup on the stirrip leather to hold it in place. She walked around the horse and raised the other stirrup. She loosened the girth. "You've made your mind up. So why don't you tell me now."

"Not sure." Margot's voice hardened. "You certainly are remarkably good. I think you've made great progress with this horse and the others of mine that you train, but I don't know that it makes you an assistant—"

"Cut it out," Sally burst in. "You just want to hog it all for yourself. I'd like to know where you would have been with Steven if I hadn't given you the idea to see Bill to claim the title of co-trainer," she spat out, tugging the reins over Thad's head. "Fine, you've got me six months. And that's it." She stomped off, roughly leading Thad toward the door.

Margot looked after her. Six months. I have six months to compel her to adore me as I adore her. Yes, I adore her, but I won't be browbeaten. I won't play Herbert to her Margot.

"Pete," she called out from the arena door. "Bring out Odds & Sods, then Miss Higgins." She was determined to ride Sally into oblivion.

Now, she sat on the rocking chair on her front porch, her gaze drifting out to the endless blackness. She was dressed in gray sweatpants, sneakers, and a bottle green sweatshirt. Ed was next to her, propped up against the door, his knees bent before him.

He'd dropped by, they'd had the pizza he'd placed on the backseat of his Jaguar, and then, at his urging because the fall night was unexpectedly warm, he'd suggested they sit outside, talking and listening.

Margot felt exhausted, yet she yearned for that lustful ardor that he made so special. That burning passion that she'd never felt except when he placed her under his dominion with his slaps and lashes. And yet, she was tired. She still seemed to ache from their last meeting. She felt drained by her conversation with Sally and Steven's return with his two horses and the hopes that seemed to simultaneously grow and then crash to pieces.

She sighed, suddenly seeking that release. "Tired of star gazing?" she asked.

"You mean black night gazing," Ed responded, turning toward her.

"Come here," Margot stretched out her hand to him. He took it and stood. She pulled herself up and guided him to the rocking chair. She felt that urge in her center just by standing next to him. He sat in the chair, his feet before him, rocking to and fro. Margot fell to her knees and unzipped him, pulling his flaccid member from his pants.

"Hi, little guy," she breathed to him, nibbling the tip. Even as she did so, her own juices began flowing. She fondled him with her mouth and tongue, but to no avail. Slowly, he rhythmically began to rock, all the while Margot following with her mouth. But it was fruitless.

"What *is* the matter?" she asked irritably, breaking away.

But Ed said nothing, merely continued his even rocking in nonchalance. A slow understanding dawned on Margot. Perhaps the *only* way he could be roused was by beating her. She sighed and stood. She yearned to be taken. She yearned for the pulsating heat that she'd felt with no others. And yet, she felt too tired to withstand the beatings. She was still too bludgeoned from the other night.

She didn't want to go through the ordeal, but she craved him when he was hard. "Come *on*," she said crossly. She swung the screen door open as Ed followed her inside.

"What's in here?" She bent to look in the canvas bag he'd brought, the one she knew he carried his tennis rackets and tennis shoes in. "Playing tennis tonight, sport?"

But tonight it held only the familiar leather strap and the clothesline. Gingerly, she lifted them out. She held them both at arms length, peering at them. Funny how two such innocuous artifacts could carry so much weight and meaning.

She sighed, turning to gaze at him. She smiled. He looked so foolish, his feeble member hanging outside his pants when she had angrily left it in frustration. Oh well, she sighed to herself. She supposed she must withstand the pain for the tremendous gain.

She led the way to her bedroom, swiftly locking the door in case tonight were the night a groom should decide to visit. Determinedly, she strode to the windows, pulling the shades down. Wouldn't *that* be the last straw if someone saw her getting beaten to smithereens?

She turned, hands on her hips, to face Ed. Tall, glamorous Ed with his limp penis. What a laugh, she thought rather churlishly. He can't get it up even a little.

"What do you want to do?" She shrugged, her voice exasperated.

He glanced at the paraphrenalia in her hands. Obediently, she held them out to him. A sudden vision of her own naked body writhing in his mirror filled her with total desire. She'd take what he wanted her to have. For the indignity and the pain only heightened the lust. She heaved a breath of resignation and desire.

But then, just as she held out the equipment, she pulled them back. Perhaps, maybe the tables could turn.

"Go to the bureau," she commanded gently. Submissively, he obeyed her, as if in penance for his failure. "You can watch yourself." Margot reached around him, unbuttoning his fly, pulling his jeans and his underwear to the floor. Quickly, she pulled her own off, and stood behind him, now both naked from the waist down.

And then, with scarcely a thought, she raised the leather strap and brought it down on his buttocks. He flinched, his muscles tightening on the sides of his behind. Again, she brought it down. He clutched at the sides of the bureau, grunting.

Margot raised her arm, glancing at herself in the mirror. She hesitated a moment; disbelief that she would do such things stayed her hand. But she was attracted. She liked seeing her strong bicep muscles reflected in the mirror with her arm raised as she held the strap.

Fearfully, Margot glanced at him in the mirror. A smile of satisfaction was plastered to his face. And below, peering above the bureau, stood his upright penis. The sight inspired her. She let her own desire mount, for soon he would be hers, after all. She lowered her arm hard. As she smacked him, she saw him recoil, watched his buttocks tighten. Her own cavity grew even more moist with lust.

He grunted out her name. Margot placed the leather on the bed behind her and swatted him with the flat of her hand. It stung her, but the sting was followed by intense pleasure. She felt her body tense with anticipation. She saw his breath come heavily.

"Again?" she questioned between clenched teeth.

He groaned an answer, gripping the bureau. Again, Margot smacked him. She turned back toward the leather but, spying the rope, she gathered a new idea. She picked it up and began wrapping it tightly about his buttocks and upper thighs, winding it ever higher, leaving only his hard, throbbing rod exposed, as the rope finally ended at his hips. He was firmly encased in a girdle of rope.

Fascinated, she watched the area redden with the constraint, watched him convulsively sway forward and back. Margot's own body reeled with passion at the sight til she thought she could no longer stand it. Rapidly, she spun him around, roughly guided him to the bed, and wildly threw herself on top of him, still bound, wriggling and panting for her. ----

CHAPTER 15

"I'm leaving." Sally announced. "I'm giving two weeks notice."

Margot stared at her angrily, the Norelco coffee maker separating them a they stood side by side in the tack room peering through the glass window at the horse that Pete was lunging.

"That's not the deal." Her throat constricted. "You said you'd give me two weeks to make up my mind. You've given me two days and two weeks notice."

"But you were just stalling." Sally's voice remained friendly, easy, as if she were discussing the day's marketing list. "You'd keep stringing me along."

"Where are you going?" Margot wanted to say, You said you'd stick around a few months as a groom. You didn't say you'd stick around a couple days. But that sounded as if she were sniveling. She wouldn't snivel.

"Rob's." Sally shrugged.

Margot jerked imperceptively. Rob was her friend. They had an unwritten rule not to steal one another's help.

"He didn't steal me," Sally responded, as if reading her thoughts. "I told him I was leaving, and if I didn't go there, I'd go somewhere else."

Margot pursued her lips. Sally was too aggressive for her place. Margot would have to watch her back all the time, make sure she didn't get the rug pulled from under her. Why in the world did she even think about keeping Sally? She swallowed. Unfortunately, she knew the answer: if Sally were her faithful employee, the two of them would be brilliant together. The question was: how to make her faithful.

"Anyway," Sally purred, sipping the black coffee, "if I'm at Rob's, which isn't so far away, you'll have ample opportunity to win me back."

"Is he making you assistant trainer?"

"Of course not," Sally said sharply. "But if I leave, maybe you will."

Margot merely stared, speechless, at the vixen before her. I thought I was tough, she huffed, but nothing like this little thing. She turned and headed out the door. "Look, Sally, why don't you leave now. Pack your bags, and be out by noon."

"Oh, no," she wailed, "but my job doesn't start for two weeks. I told him two weeks. He can't take me before then."

"Why in the world would I let you hang out here when you've just dumped me? I don't need to waste a paycheck on you anymore." Margot glared. "Get your stuff out in one hour. I'll be up to check."

Now, an hour later, as she strode up the hill toward the grooms' quarters she pondered her haste. Had she been too impetuous? Of course she'd find another groom, but did she really want one? Had she lost a lot by getting rid of Sally? She clambered up the stairs and knocked lightly at the door.

Easy come, easy go, she thought, opening it, without waiting for an answer. Steven leaves, Steven returns, Sally leaves. Someone else comes. The room was devoid of the familiar photos and horse statues that Sally had placed around it. The coat closet door was open and bare. Margot glanced into the kitchen. It was tidy, everything in order.

On the bed lay Sally's huge suitcase, packed with her gear. Her saddle sat on the floor, propped against the wall. Margot peered into the closet, also empty. "Sally?"

"In the bathroom. Just a minute."

Moments later, the door opened, and Sally walked out, in a long wool skirt, boots laced to her ankles and a long gray knit sweater. Margot's heart lurched at the sight of her. She was so ladylike and beguiling.

"Where are you going?"

"My friend Becky's just out of town. She's picking me up soon." Sally was strangely quiet. Somehow, the perkiness in her voice and her gait had disappeared.

"Do you think you were precipitous in giving notice?" Margot asked, feeling rather school marmish as she asked that question. She sat on the edge of the bed which Sally had stripped.

"No. You got to be, in order to make your way in this world." Her words echoed Margot's very own thoughts most of the time. Not this time.

Margot licked her lips. Sally's gay laughter and serious intensity would be missed. But now there was nothing more to say. "Well," Margot said brightly, standing, "I think we've said it all."

Sally walked over and lifted her face toward Margot's. Then, without waiting, she leaned forward and pressed her lips to Margot's cheek.

"I'm sorry it's ending this way," she said softly. "I really am. But I have things to accomplish. I hope you understand."

Almost frantically, Margot reached out and took Sally to her. They clasped one another in a tight embrace.

But just as suddenly as Sally had stepped up to her, she stepped back, leaving Margot alone, and forlorn.

"Just wanted to thank you," Sally said glibly, as if this hadn't happened. She hoisted the suitcase into her left hand and reached down for the saddle. "Bye." She said airily.

Margot stared after her, too stupefied at her gullibility and her bereavement to reply. Sally was gone. Sally had titillated her, lured her on with the knowledge that she would dump her just as soon as Margot responded with heat. She was shocked at her own stupidity, even as she placed her hand to her heart, feeling it pump feverishly with expectation.

For in Margot's vision, she saw herself furiously pulling off Sally's clothes, placing her gently on the bed, and sitting over her, admiring each part of her body: the swells of her fleshy breasts with the dusky ends, the indentation of her fine waist, the roundness of her hips, the length and shape of her thighs and calves. Instead, she was left with nothing. Ruefully, she looked down at her own crotch, alone and heated with frustrated expectation.

Margot sighed, beleaguered by lingering thoughts of Malcolm and new, penetrating ones of Sally. She'd probably have to give Rob a call and see what was going on, see how she could entice Sally back to her farm.

"OK, Steven, that was great. You're doing a totally great job!" Margot called out to her student from the

140

center of the arena where she stood, watching him canter through a complicated 4′ high course of jumps.

"Too bad I couldn't do it in Harrisburg," he complained, bringing his High Flyer to a walk.

"Well, you have Meadowlands. And, frankly, that's got a lot more prestige. So you saved the best one." Margot reassured him. They hadn't referred back to his weeks with Bill, his weeks away from her, but she knew she'd become his mainstay, his crutch, that he couldn't perform without her, his lucky talisman.

"My dad said he'd stop by and watch me."

Margot shot a glance into the waiting room. There, peering out the window, was Malcolm. "He's here now."

Steven nodded. "But I didn't want to tell you beforehand. Didn't want to make you nervous."

"*Me?* What about you?"

Steven shrugged, as he walked his horse about, cooling her off. "I'm used to it." As Corey walked into the arena, Steven handed him the reins and walked toward the waiting room with Margot. But he didn't go in. Only Margot did.

"Hello, Mr. Forsythe," she smiled, as if they didn't have a past. "He did a nice job, didn't he?"

"Very," he answered curtly. "You'll be taking him to the National Horse Show?"

Margot caught herself, cautioning herself to be steady. "It's up to you. I'm indifferent."

"*Indifferent?* If that's the case, perhaps I should call Bill Wainright in."

"You tried already. That didn't work. Look Mr.

Forsythe, as I may have mentioned, I find you rather coarse, rather callous, rather cruel. But I'll do the job, because I like your son." She turned, heading for the door.

She felt his hand, hard on hers, on the doorknob. "I think we'd better come to a more satisfactory agreement."

"Take your hands off me," she said clearly, her voice steely hard. "I don't want *anything* to do with your body, either."

"Ah, I see. I upset you when I alluded to your sexual prowess. My comments cut to the quick. You view yourself as surpassing your rivals in both riding ability and sexual agility. I undermined them both."

Sudden, fierce anger swelled through her. She bit her lip to keep from slamming her hand across his face. "Mr. Forsythe," Margot turned around, facing him. Venom laced her words. "I suspect that anything you say will be able to undermine me. I think you have a facile, though bitter, tongue. But I believe, if we were to strip away those words, leaving you just to your brains and your body, you couldn't hold a candle to me."

She stopped, her chest heaving with the exertion of challenging him. "Now, once again, get out. You remain odious to me."

Malcolm was silent. Finally he spoke. "Margot," his tone was soft, conciliatory. "Once again we've gotten off on the wrong foot. I apologize for ever thinking you seduced my son. And I apologize also for letting you somehow believe that I was interested in screwing you. I'm not, never have been, probably never will be." Malcolm stood.

Margot's lip curled with disgust. There was always a double-edged thrust to his words.

"I left a check on the desk covering this month's board and training fees, and an advance on the expenses for the National Horse Show at the Meadowlands to cover grooms and stall space and hay and trailoring. Hope it's satisfactory." Malcolm walked out of the door, calling his son's name.

Margot stood staring, wondering at the smallest kernel of desire that had settled within her. Somehow his steel gray hair, his black eyes and gray eyebrows, square jaw and the crows feet about his eyes sent a fleeting desire through her. And the cat and mouse game they played—stalking, prowling—only exacerbated the physical and emotional tension. For they each desired each other the same way: by sneaking up and totally humiliating the other.

She sighed, listening to the Forsythes walk down the aisle of the barn, hearing Steven call out his farewells til tomorrow. Strangely, no matter how she seemed to win with Malcolm, he always seemed to win better.

She shook her head, blotting out the thoughts. For now, she had to interview a groom to replace Sally. His name was Ricky, and he was short and stocky and already balding in his youthful early twenties. She admired the curly blond hair that wrapped around his ears, and the tuft of blond hair peering through the top of his flannel shirt, and the cute upturned nose, innocent blue eyes and wide smile. Not bad, though no match for Sally.

He looked strong, competent, and well-meaning.

Margot nodded to herself as she hired him. She'd see the extent of his competence in a few days.

"I think you'll do," she heaved, sliding off him. She'd visited him in his quarters, giving him his first pay check, reviewing the procedures of the barn. Then, when they were done talking and they stood, Margot walked up to him. Without a word, she unbuttoned his smooth shirt.

He stepped back surprised, his brows raised in wonderment.

"It goes with the turf," she whispered, pulling at the tuft of hair at his neck with her teeth, as she reached down to touch his member. Within seconds, it had stiffened, and Ricky had placed his massive hands on her breasts under the white turtleneck. Her ends hardened immediately at his touch. Then, quickly, he'd undressed her, pulled off his own clothes, and led her to the bed.

Rolling, fumbling, caressing, they'd humped each other til, finally, Margot pulled off. After all, she thought, enough is enough. I'm still his boss.

CHAPTER 16

"Corey, is there enough hay in the trailer? Pete, check that all the tack is there, including a couple extra bridles and bits. Also, make sure there's black string for me to braid their manes and tails." Margot marched from groom to groom, handing each a list of items to check before they loaded Steven Forsythe's two horses and headed to the National Horse Show.

Margot's skin prickled with excitement. Steven was riding beautifully, with an inspiration she hadn't seen before his father had removed him from the premises. He had confidence and grace. She suspected he was so thrilled to be back that he was pushing himself harder than ever.

"I'll drive the trailer. I suspect it'll take us about three hours. Pete, you ride with me." Corey, Craig and Ricky would stay at the farm, managing it in her several-day absence. Rob had said he'd come by to keep a more practiced eye. Margot spun around. "OK, let's load 'em."

Corey led High Flyer down the aisle and easily up the ramp of the two-horse trailer, then attached him to the cross ties. Margot ran the chain across the back of his stall. She stood at the foot of the trailer as Ricky brought Propriety, Steven's hunter, down the aisle. While he'd probably ride High Flyer, Margot needed the insurance of a backup in case something happened—lameness, colic—to the horse.

Propriety balked at the ramp, pulling back. Margot walked behind him, placing a hand on his rump. He pulled back, dragging Ricky.

"OK, Ricky, turn him around, start over." Margot stood back, watching as Ricky led the horse down the aisle, turned him and headed toward the ramp of the trailer again.

High Flyer contentedly ate his hay, oblivious to the commotion about him. As they neared the ramp, Propriety again pulled back, but Margot stood behind him, her hand on his rump, as if to push him up.

145

"Craig, give me a hand."

Craig came up on Propriety's other side, placing a hand on his rump also. But the horse sidestepped, again placing himself off center to the ramp.

"Let's start over." Margot glanced at her watch. She hadn't planned on this. Propriety rarely had difficulty loading. "Corey, get some grain."

Now Corey stood at the top of the ramp holding a bucket of grain, while Margot and Craig stood at the bottom on either side of the ramp, and Ricky led him. Ricky turned the horse and led him forward again. Margot pulled a short crop from the rear pocket of her jeans and gently tapped the horse. Pete followed up closely behind him, giving him no easy option but to go forward to the waiting grain in the black rubber bucket.

As soon as Propriety had entered the trailer, Margot stepped forward, fastening the chain. As soon as Craig and Ricky slipped underneath, Margot and Pete lifted the metal doors of the navy trailer and slid the bolts. She peered in, pleased to see both horses contentedly munching the hay, as if there had never been a to-do.

"I guess we're ready to roll, aren't we?" Margot breathed deeply, feeling her adrenalin pump through her body, as she hopped into the navy truck that would haul the trailer. Steven would meet her at the show.

Nodding and waving amid the cries of good luck, she and Pete slowly headed down the dirt drive, past the still green pastures, the grazing horses nibbling at whatever grass remained. At the far barn, the barn on the corner of the property where she stored grain and hay and stall bedding, Margot peered up at the grain bin, full to brimming, and at the hay bales stacked higher than the windows, and smiled with satisfaction. All was well.

Pete stayed in the small tack room at the horse show, his bed a small cot. The bridles, saddles, whips, lunge lines and clothing hung about him. On a small shelf, he'd placed the hoof polish, the Showsheen and the braiding material. His job was to watch over the horses in the two stalls next to him.

Margot was in a motel just down the street. Steven was in the same motel, floors away. She had made sure of that. She wanted no sign of improper behavior, she thought, as she stepped out of a shower before going to bed.

Tomorrow, she and Steven would work the horses. Sunday, Steven would ride one or the other. At last. She hadn't been part of the Nationals scene since she had ridden and placed within the Top Ten. Now it was Steven's turn. Then it would be Marcy and Jenny's turn. It had, after all, worked out all right. Harrisburg had been a trial run. Her past tribulations didn't seem to matter anymore, now that she was here.

She smiled grimly, ready to acknowledge that sometimes the tribulations of the past sweetened the events of the present. Perhaps that had been Malcolm Forsythe's gift to her, she thought wryly. He was cutting her a break, after all.

Margot started as the phone rang. She reached across the double bed to answer it, flipping her long wet hair behind her ears.

"My dad wants to know if you'll have breakfast

with us tomorrow," Steven suggested tentatively.

"Yes, if you'll eat at 5:00. I have to work the horses by 6:00, my schedule time."

"Um, that's early for him. Fine for me. I'll call you back."

Margot didn't suggest breakfast alone with Steven. For Malcolm would take that opportunity to chastise her for seducing his son again. But when Steven called back, he called to say they'd meet at five in the coffee shop.

Glancing at the small brown clock above the cashier's desk, Margot sipped her coffee and ate the cinnamon toast before her. It was 5:20, but the Forsythes hadn't arrived. She had to leave in ten minutes. Then Steven was to join her at 6:30, his turn on the course. Would Malcolm bristle that she hadn't waited? She wanted to be terribly accommodating, fearing that the slightest infraction would cause him to pull out his son, or at least upset him. But she couldn't wait. She couldn't risk upsetting her schedule, the horses' schedules or the horse show's schedule.

She shook her head ruefully. That Malcolm, always toying with the system, trying to see how far he could bend her before she broke.

At last, she stood, hastily scribbling a note, telling Steven where to meet her, and handed it to the cashier. She made no apologies for leaving.

"Ah, Margot, there you are," Malcolm's hearty voice resounded behind her as she lifted some bills from her red leather wallet. "Sorry we're late, but so, apparently, are you."

"No," she answered sharply. "I'm just leaving. We

had a 5:00 breakfast, and breakfast is over."

"Certainly you can delay your busy schedule," his voice was tinged with sarcasm.

"As a matter of fact, Mr. Forsythe, I can't. I have a schedule that must fit around the schedules of the other trainers and riders." She turned toward Steven. "Meet me there at 6:30."

Malcolm put a steadying hand on her arm. "Always distant. Always preemptory, as if you owned the world."

"On the contrary, sir," she shot back. "It is precisely because I don't own the world that I must keep to this schedule so that it fits into the schedules of those around me." She jerked her arm away, stepping forward. "If you'll excuse me."

"I daresay you could rearrange things."

"Well, maybe *you* could, but I can't."

"Then I shall," he answered shortly.

"Well, don't." Her eyes flashed with indignation. "This is my show. Don't wreck it." Margot turned on her heel and stormed out the room, chest heaving. "And don't wreck it for Steven this time, either!" She shot back over her shoulder as she marched down the corridor to the heavy doors.

He was insufferably rude and conceited, she muttered to herself. I'd like to pummel him, show him that I can't be ruled by him. I wonder what he thinks about that, *if* he thinks about that at all. He runs billions of dollars of companies and highly paid executives with more success than he runs me and my lovely little farm.

She smirked with pleasure as she zipped her leather bomber jacket against the darkness and the

149

cold morning as she headed for the truck. But she knew that as frustrated as she was by him, he was equally frustrated by her.

The day passed quickly, as she and Pete prepared the horses and Steven and themselves. The first event of Sunday morning would begin at 8:00. She and Pete would be up and about at 5:00, perhaps earlier, braiding the manes and tails, polishing their feet, smoothing their forelocks. Then she'd have a small opportunity to school the horse before Steven would ride him in the competition. She doubted, anyway, if she'd be able to sleep more than a few minutes from the tension and excitement of the upcoming day.

She looked High Flyer over, running her hand up and down his four legs, checking for any swelling or sensitivities. Everything, thank goodness, was still fine. Then she similarly checked Propriety.

Now it was time. The days of preparation had at last narrowed down to these few moments that Steven would canter about the immense arena with eight difficult jumps. All those months of training whittled down to just one chance.

Margot clasped her hands, her heart thumping as she watched Steven swing his leg over his horse, his long, muscular thighs encased in beige breeches, his calves in beautiful high black leather boots, spurs clasped to their heels. She looked up, smiled at the young man before her, in forest green tie, white shirt, forest green jacket, and black velvet huntcap.

"You can do it," she whispered, quickly squeezing his knee. "We're watching." Where, she wondered, was Malcolm? Who was with his entourage?

She clasped her hands before her again to stop

their trembling as Steven trotted High Flyer through the in gate. Hardly daring to breathe, she watched him break into a canter in the opening circle and impeccably complete the course of eight brightly colored jumps. With a whoop, she turned, hugging Pete, and waited for Steven to exit.

"Great job," she hugged him as he slid to the ground. Pete took the horse, leading him back to his stall.

She turned back to the ring to watch the remaining riders, trying to gauge from each ride whether Steven would make the cut. At last, hours later, the announcement came. Steven, number fourteen, would be returning for the final ride-off. Beaming, she squeezed his hand.

"Come on, let's have lunch and watch the show in some regular seats til it's your turn. There are a lot of events between now and then." Margot turned to Pete in the tack room. "You OK?"

"Yup."

She nodded. Funny, how in this situation neither ever exceeded the accepted practices of trainer and groom. Vaguely, as she and Steven made their way to seats, she wondered how many other trainers screwed their grooms.

Malcolm offered reserved praise, but never introduced Margot to the woman next to him. She had blonde, meticulously coiffed hair that fell to her shoulders. Her high cheekbones were well rouged and well oiled, her almond-shaped eyes were enhanced by black eye shadow. She carelessly sat on her black mink coat.

Margot squirmed imperceptively feeling like a hick

from the farm next to her. No wonder Malcolm didn't introduce her. No wonder he treated Margot as he did when he escorted the likes of this woman around.

So, Margot thought, that's why he's not interested in the likes of me. I couldn't possibly compare to that lady in her sophistication and her jewelery. I probably could fuck his eyes out, but I'd never look as glamorous. Even as she thought that, a slight tingling settled between her legs. Despite everything, Malcolm was somehow horribly compelling.

Margot looked at her watch. At last it was time. She nudged Steven. "Come on."

Steven stood, picking up his hunt cap on his lap before him.

"Good luck, Steven," his father called out as they traipsed out of the box seats, stepping over paper cups of soda and boxes of popcorn that now lay strewn about the cement floor.

They returned to the stalls. High Flyer was on crossties, ready.

Again, Margot stood with Pete at the side of the ring, her eyes narrowed in concentration as she watched Steven enter the ring yet again. Unknowingly, she gripped Pete tightly by the forearm.

Together, with the other trainers and students, Margot and Steven had walked the newly configured course of eight jumps. They were walking the strides, determining how many the horse could take before each jump, and determining precisely how the rider should maneuver the horse to make the strides and take the jumps.

She wanted to take Pete's hand, have his warmth

against her frozen fingers, feel an ally among all the competitors. For, though she knew them all, there were no friends among them. How, when the stakes were so high, could there be?

She breathed deeply and shut her eyes for one moment in brief prayer as Steven trotted into the ring, remembering when she pretended to convince herself that it didn't matter whether or not she took Steven to the National Horse Show; that it was no big deal, since she'd have other students here next year. She'd thought that she already had a fine reputation. But, now, as she stood, gripping her hands tightly together, she knew it did matter.

It mattered as much for Steven, as it did for her. Six years of intense work were wrapped up in these five minutes. And countless glorious years of her future were wrapped up here also. Yes, she admitted, Steven's performance mattered to her. No matter how many horses she trained and sold, no matter how many customers clamored for her, today mattered almost more than anything else she had ever done.

And, when with relief, Steven executed a perfect round, Margot threw her arms around Pete, clapped her hands together and felt tears well up in her eyes. He'd been brilliant. And when the judge lined up the ten riders, and Steven was among them, she could barely keep the tears from overflowing. And, finally, when Steven was proclaimed the best junior rider in America, Margot let the tears of pride and relief wash down her cheeks.

CHAPTER 17

Margot was exultant as she sipped the champagne before her. Now, late at night, they had gathered — she, Steven, Malcolm and his sultry blonde, Steven's mother and her husband — in Malcolm's suite celebrating the success.

A tin of caviar, toast points and bits of egg and onion sat before them on the coffee table. Malcolm had had someone chauffeur the dainties from New York City to celebrate his son's success.

Despite the probable factions, conversation flowed easily, though Steven's stepfather was quieter than the others, clearly uncomfortable in Malcolm's presence. His mother exuded effervesance and charm. She too rode horses, and in fact Margot could practically see this pixyish woman in her short hairdo, freckled upturned nose in high boots and breeches.

"And now, Margot, what are your plans?" Malcolm suddenly asked, turning to her for the first time.

She shrugged, tossing her heavy hair. "Now get my other students here next year."

"And what do you suggest for Steven?"

Margot tensed. "He knows his options. It's for you two to discuss."

"Oh?" Malcolm raised a quizzical eye.

"He can try for the Olympics. He can quit riding. And options in between. I did one of the in-between options," she smiled, again sipping from her glass. Carefully, she placed it on the wooden coffee table before them, sensing that the mood of the party was going to change toward a subtle hostility perhaps aimed at herself.

Margot leaned forward. "Thank you for this little soirée. But I didn't get much sleep last night." She stood and headed for the door, nodding to the assembled family members.

"Let me escort you to your room. It is the least I can do after the accolades that you have helped Steven garner." Malcolm stood, and before she could decline, he had joined her in the corridor.

Her throat constricted as slight tremors seemed to tweak her, when they stopped in front of her door. Nervously, she inserted the key into the lock, pushing the door open. She turned to face Malcolm. "Why, thanks for the escort," she made an effort to sound perky. But she felt trembly.

Malcolm stepped in, closing the door behind him. "I wanted to thank you," he replied gruffly. He reached for her shoulders pulling her toward him, bent down and roughly kissed her, pressing his lips firmly against hers as she struggled to break away. His tongue pried open her sealed lips, thrusting deeply into the moist cavern. At length, he released her.

She fell back against the wall, gasping, her hand across her heart as pangs of heat coursed through her.

"Are you legs as tightly locked as your mouth?" He asked, his voice tinged with sarcasm.

"How dare you," she lashed out. "How dare you come near me!" She raised her hand and swiftly smacked it against his cheek in a stinging blow. The sound resonated in the small room.

Again, he pulled her toward him, pushing her head back on her neck, pressing his lips against hers, thrusting his tongue between them. With his other hand, he pressed against her breast in small, rotating motions.

Horrified, Margot raised her knee and slammed it into his groin. He released her and doubled over, grabbing at himself, grunting as he clutched his stomach. "Damn," he scowled, his face contorted with pain.

"I hate you," she said, turning away, chest heaving. But a kind of thrill swam over her, a kind of titillation that she felt when she and Ed were together wafted through her limbs. "And you deserve it. You deserve it for your behavior just now and for your behavior of the past few months."

"I didn't think I needed a teacher," he muttered.

But Margot didn't need him. Instead she walked over to the bed and lifted her mystery novel in apparent unconcern. "When you're done pampering yourself, Mr. Forsythe, you're welcome to leave." Her voice was laced with sarcasm, as her eyes scanned the lines of the book searching for a familiar place to begin reading.

Malcolm didn't answer. But she heard him rustling about. Curiously, she raised her head. Now he stood upright, as if nothing had happened. Moments later he walked over to her. "Please accept my apologies," he said softly, standing above her by the side of the bed. "The evening robbed me of my senses."

"Why don't you screw your blonde?" she asked, surprised at the bitterness in her voice.

"I will. But I thought I'd kiss you too." He bent down and held out a hand. "A gesture of friendship?" He asked somewhat tentatively.

She took it, and clasped it between her palms. She looked at him searchingly. Suddenly, she wanted them to be friends. She didn't want to be manipulated by him, but she didn't want the enmity either. She was tired of fighting him. And at last she believed he had seen that he had met his match in her, just as she had met hers.

With a sudden, tired relief, she smiled up at him, as tears flooded her eyes. She swallowed, in an effort to quell them. But it was too late. He had seen. He nodded sympathetically.

"Look, let's just call all this quits," she offered, her voice muffled by the tears. "We can put it behind us. It's over now. Steven won. He'll leave me to go on to college and other things. You and I won't see each other again. But let's leave as friends."

And one day, she thought, suddenly wistful, you and I might be able to—she swallowed—come together.

"All right." He stood up straight, withdrawing his hand from her clasp.

Margot scrambled off the bed, dropping her book to the floor. She faced him, but as he stepped forward again, she backed away swiftly. "Friends," she repeated. He would not have her body yet, she vowed.

It was time to see Rob. Sally had been there almost a month. She wanted to see how the girl fared, see if perhaps there were a chance to lure her back, see if, perhaps, Sally had grown any fonder of her.

The fall nights darkened early. The equinox

approached, scarcely three weeks away, so the night was pitch without even a semblance of a moon to steer her. With only the high beams of her jeep to guide her over the frozen rutty roads, Margot drove past the small farm houses, large pastures and paddocks to Rob's.

She headed for the log cabin. She'd told him she'd be by that evening after work. She heard the anticipation in his voice, and thrilled at the thought of his touch on her. For, really, he had an inventive, sensual way. They could last for hours together. She girded herself for a long night of kisses and caresses, and planned a light day tomorrow, so she'd have a long night with him. She smiled at the thought of her imminent arousal.

But as she stepped upon the porch, placed her hand on the knob of the screen door, her heart tumbled. She knew she'd made a gross mistake.

For, there, before the fire was Sally, naked in her lithe beauty, kneeling before Rob, also naked, his stiff sword buried up to the hilt in her mouth. Sally's hands fondled his testicles and buttocks while he delicately traced imaginary lines on her shoulders and hair.

Hypnotized, Margot stopped, eyes wide with disbelief and jealousy. So, Sally would do it with him and not with her. What had he promised her? Had she become assistant trainer, then? Or was this how Sally planned to become assistant trainer? It never occurred to her that Sally might have liked Rob, for Margot knew that Sally gave nothing for free.

Margot grasped at the door knob as she watched Sally's tongue lazily wind about his rod, as if festooning it with ribbons. She clutched at her stomach, pressing against the sudden, ripe knot of anguish in its pit. She swallowed, as an unquenchable jealousy assaulted her. Without thinking, she pulled at the screen door, and pushed at the wooden door.

Rob and Sally didn't move—a still life, entitled, "Woman Performs Fellatio on Man." They merely stared at her, stunned by the intrusion. Margot stood, a smirk across her face. She'd show Sally she didn't really care, that it was nothing, after all, to her. Sally could do what she wanted to achieve her ends.

"Please, don't stop," she said smoothly, settling herself down on the Shaker chair in front of the fire, where she could gaze at them.

Rob tried to pull away, but Sally was straight business. Her lips would not relinguish their hold. She batted her lashes subtly at Margot, and returned to her concerns.

"Oh, Margot, this is embarrassing," Rob muttered, his desire seemingly dissipated. He tried to place his hands over his member and Sally's mouth as if to shield them from view.

"It's no problem, really," Margot rejoined airily. "I've got lots of time." She gloated at his embarrassment, and wondered why Sally lacked any. Deep inside, her heart ached that he would so easily abandon her for Sally, and fury that Sally would behave so wantonly with Rob. How long had they been doing this? How many nights? Night after night? Had it begun the first day she arrived? Margot ground her fist into her stomach.

Sally lightly drummed her fingers on his backside, trying to regain Rob's attention, as her tongue and lips rolled over his shaft. Suddenly, he seemed to have forgotten Margot and his embarrassment. He came to life again, stiffening, grasping at her shoulders, lurching forward and back as she played her music upon him. He shut his eyes.

Margot was stymied for even when he professed embarrassment, he didn't stop.

Her senses rolled til she thought she'd explode. Despair, anger and passion clawed at her. She crossed her legs, pressing her thighs together to stop the ache in her crotch. She heard her own breath come heavily, even as she heard Rob moan and speed his breathing.

He reached down, lifting Sally's breasts, enfolding them in his hands, massaging them as Sally toyed with him. Margot licked her lips, a sudden vision of Sally pressing her mouth against her own snatch. She gasped with longing at her vision. Sally gave her a sidelong glance, without releasing him.

But at length as his moans of feverish passion subsided, she did, lapping up his remains as she turned, grinning to Margot.

"Hi, good to see you," she said casually, standing, her perky breasts aglow, her slim hips tantalizing.

"Uh, Sal, I think you should go." Rob reached for his pants.

"No, hurry, Rob," Margot said standing. She yearned to yank Sally's hair out and kiss her til her lips bled from the pressure. How dare she take one of my men? How dare she screw someone I screw?

"I'm still looking for a groom." Margot said

160

lightly, trying to keep control. She longed to run hard hands over the girl's body, stab her with kisses.

"No deal."

Margot shrugged. "No deal, then."

As the door shut behind her, Margot turned to Rob. Keep your temper, she warned herself. You don't own him. You never said you were coming over to screw him. She smiled to cover the hurt and the frustration that threatened to boil over.

"So, you ready for me?" She winked.

He glanced down at his pants covering his spent member. "Not yet."

Anger ripped through Margot. She wasn't going to take sloppy seconds in any case. She wasn't going to have anyone do *her* favors. And she most definitely wasn't going to follow in Sally's footsteps.

"See you around, Rob." Angrily, she stomped out of the room and back to her car, ignoring his calls. There was nothing he could do for her anymore. She'd never get him to forego Sally, nor help her lure Sally back to her own farm. He must've figured out what an outstanding trainer she was going to be, and he must have figured out how cheery she was. And he'd obviously figured out that she gave head.

What I really ought to do, Margot grimaced as she sped up Route 41 toward the farm, was barge in on Sally and just take her. Instead, she pulled over at the corner gas station and called Ed.

She felt like a rousing beating.

CHAPTER 18

Roses? A dozen white roses? Margot had ripped open the card. From Malcolm. How—she had searched for a right word—suspicious. On the one hand, he seemed to be mending his ways. She had smiled happily, a she zipped up her chaps. On the other hand, asking his secretary to order roses for someone didn't require too much effort. But, as Margot plumped them up in a glass vase in her bedroom, she accepted them gratefully.

And now, today, a box of wonderfully rich chocolates from Godiva. What was he doing to her? Obviously trying to seduce her. The cards said nothing, beside his name. Dryly, she wondered if he even signed them himself. Or if he kept a stack of already-signed cards in his right desk drawer which his secretary pulled out each time she sent flowers to an unsuspecting victim.

Margot hugged herself, grateful to be wooed by so smooth a man, and then swung her leg over Miss Higgins. She'd have to hurry, for when Malcolm called earlier, he'd asked if she'd meet him at the Italian restaurant for dinner. She knew she didn't want to turn this invitation down.

He was waiting in the far booth, the one Herbert and she usually shared, in an open-necked white business shirt, but no tie, and a maroon v-neck sweater. Margot slid into the banquette, across from him, pulling her calf-length black herringbone wool dress down.

"Thanks for inviting me for dinner," she beamed.

Even so, a small voice warned her to be careful. She didn't know of what to be careful, but just to be careful.

"Wanted to begin our relationship on a new footing. Steven, as you know, is retiring from active competition and is going off to New Hampshire for college."

"Seems a shame to be so wonderful a rider and forsake it," she murmured, sipping the glass of wine proffered by the waitress.

"There are other things in life. Even *you* would have to agree to that," his voice was soft, his comment was pointed.

She nodded. "I would. But for me, nothing else compared. Nothing else thrilled me and gave me as much joy and satisfaction as horses. But for Steven, I'd say, at the very least, he needs to find out what else is out there."

Did his leg purposely brush against hers? She moved her own, suddenly suspecting. But dinner passed easily, and she accepted his offer to return to his home for a nightcap. She followed him in her jeep.

"This is gorgeous," she breathed, as they drove up a wide manicured mile-long dirt road, lined on one side by split-rail fencing, on the other by carefully scattered boulders. The sprawling single-level house, built around an enormous round swimming pool, topped a mountain. She parked her jeep on the circular driveway, overlooking the tennis court and a stable with paddocks.

"Steven's horses go there," Malcolm nodded. "My caretaker will oversee them, until Steven can bear to part from them."

Margot nodded silently. She walked past marble statues of thoroughbreds to an immense front hall. Large modern sculptures of things she couldn't discern seemed to stand stoically in the large rooms.

"This is beautiful," she gushed, feeling as if she were being swept off her feet to some fantasy land of white stone and marble. "Did you build it up here?"

"No. I found the land after it was built. So I just had it moved," he replied casually, not giving it another thought. "Then, of course, we built the barns and tennis court." He helped her off with her suede jacket, and taking her elbow, steered her into a navy and mahogany library, the only non-white room that she could see. She gasped at the room, lined with leather-bound volumes from floor to ceiling. A rolling ladder in a far corner seemed to wait for instructions.

Margot dropped to a large, pillow-laden navy leather couch. Malcolm sat next to her, handing her a glass of burgundy wine.

He turned. "We're starting anew, aren't we?" He breathed softly, a hint of air gracing her ear.

Margot, suddenly alert, pulled back. "Sorry, I'm not for sale."

"I didn't think I bought you," he said simply, lifting her fingers to his lips. "I bought this land. I bought this house. But I don't buy people."

How comforting, she though wryly. But I don't believe you. She remained stiffly composed.

"I'm not for free either," she retorted archly.

She should go. She should stand up and leave him. But something unknown to her compelled her to stay seated, to find out where he was leading her. Maybe, if the path were attractive enough, she might follow.

"What do you think is so fantastically mystical about your body that you withhold it from me, Margot?" he whispered, leaning close, his breath searing her cheek. His hand dropped to her knee, brushing the skirt of her dress above her knee.

She inhaled sharply. "I don't want to be used. Try your blonde."

"All right, all right," he pulled back, draping both arms above him on the couch back. "I don't want to rile you."

Margot relaxed, sinking back against the pillows. But she was wary, and disappointed that he did not fight for her. Suddenly, his seduction seemed so mechanical, as if he tried with all the women on the off chance that he'd get laid.

You ought to go, she remonstrated to herself. But she couldn't force herself to leave. Yet she had no intention of having sex.

Malcolm edged closer, so that his arm lay on the couch back above her. She eyed it, letting him know that she knew precisely what his plans were.

But she was unprepared.

For, abruptly, without warning, he dropped his fingers to her ribs and tickled her. "What?" she gasped, a small burst of laughter issuing from her lips.

"Do you like this?" he smiled, as his fingers tickled her ribs more forcefully. "This is a very ticklish place, too," he whispered. His other hand came around and separated her thighs, tickling their inner folds, til she laughed helplessly. Weakly, she tried to push him away, but she had no strength.

"Oh, Malcolm, please, let me catch my breath," she gasped for air, as his fingers roamed across her ribs and her stomach, dipped to her inner thighs. Gales of laughter echoed throughout the room as Malcolm reduced her to a mass of abandoned giggles.

"Oh, Malcolm, oh, don't," she giggled, as she fell easily against the pillows, stretching her legs before her. She didn't feel him roll on top of her, didn't realize that he was unbuttoning the buttons of her herringbone dress, or running one hand from her inner thigh to her crotch.

For, still, through it all, he tickled her. Suddenly, with an alarmed start, she realized what he was doing. She tried to remove his hands, tried to break away, but the peals of laughter still broke from her, reducing her to mere slush.

He buried his face between her naked breasts, then to her nipples, as his other hand kept her weak with laughter. She tried to kick him off, but she had no energy or ability. Numbly, she felt his hand dip into the waist of her beige lace panties and drop to her crotch, fumbling with its folds.

Irritated, she again tried to pull away, but only her mind reacted. Her body was a limp mass of giddy delight, feverishly responding to his moving fingers, as he unzipped his own pants.

She heard her panties rip as he pulled at them, then vaguely saw the fabric being tossed in the air. But still she laughed, feeling his fingers knead her rib cage and her inner thighs. She gasped for air, fearing she would choke with the exhilarated laughter, but paralyzed by him.

His mouth feverishly kissed and toyed with her breasts, as one hand guided himself between her spread, pliable legs into her mound, too exhausted to fight back.

He pumped against her and she, despite herself, pumped back, writhing in a giddy whorl of giggles, as he kissed her lips and nose, cheeks and ears, mouthed her nipples and massaged her breasts, tickling her ribs, until he had thoroughly hammered her.

Satiated, he broke away, smiling, himself laughing. But it took Margot long moments to gain control. Gasping, she lay on the couch, legs splayed, dress unfastened, wondering if she had come or been tickled to death. Then, the haze ended, and she realized what he had done.

She pushed herself up. "Why did you do that?" Her eyes blazed at the insult, but her body glowed from the passionate embrace.

"You needed it."

"Needed what?" She ground her teeth in anger.

"Needed to get banged." He shifted his weight and modestly dressed himself.

"I *get* banged." In a huff, she pulled her dress down and cross her arms to cover her breasts.

"No, no I'm afraid not, Margot," Malcolm said kindly, zipping his fly. "You bang. You don't *get* banged."

"How dare you," she sputtered, sitting upright. "This is my body."

"I was looking for a little less conceit about that body." Malcolm stood, wandering over to a far window.

"You have no right to look for *any*thing about my

body."

"Did you like it?" He turned toward her. "Ahh," he said sadly, as she began to button her dress. "Don't cover your breasts. They're lovely, just lovely. They're firm, supple, well-shaped." He shook his head, as if in remorse.

"Shut *up!*" She stomped out of the room. "I'm leaving." She grabbed her jacket from the front-hall closet.

"Oh, Margot," he followed her, his voice low and soothing. Did it mock her also, she wondered. "Don't leave. We were just beginning. Margot," he whispered, coming up behind her as she fumbled with the brass doorknob. "You are just beautiful. Your thighs are strong, long-limbed. Your stomach is taut, your behind is soft but firm. You are a delicacy." His eyes gleamed.

"You repulse me," she spat out, pulling fiercely at the door. "Help me. Open this," she ordered, stamping her foot in frustrated anger. How humiliating to be unable to leave under the barrage of insults.

Malcolm leaned around her and easily opened the door. "*Au revoir, ma petite,*" he called.

Only when she'd driven away from the house, beginning her descent from the mountain, did she relax, her fury somehow subsiding into a delicious remembrance of his strong, knowing hands on her body, his passionate mouth on hers, his hard member within her. She bit her lip.

For the first time, she really didn't know how to behave, or what to feel. Well, then, she just wouldn't think about him. He was bound to go away.

But the question echoed, as she drove the lonely

168

roads. Did she like it? Yes, she did like it. She liked it very much. But she'd never, never do it with him again. Unless *she* were in charge. She thought she remembered him, but as she mulled over their embrace, she realized that she scarcely remembered it.

What, in fact, were those lips like? And his hands? Were they long and thin? Or stubby? Hairy or hairless? What did his penis look like? His chest?

I guess that was the teaser, the preview at the movies, she mused, pulling into her own driveway. The lone outdoor light shined invitingly. If I liked it, I get more. But, the question remains, will he make me pay for it as Sally would? Or is it free? What strings are attached?

Margot switched off the outside light, turned on the upstairs hall light, and meandered up her stairs. She was exhausted, as exhausted as if she'd been with Ed. It was the same actually, what Ed and Malcolm had done to her. They'd subjugated her, reduced her to a pleading, useless pulp.

She stripped off her clothes, placing them in the laundry basket and stepped inside the shower, pulling the door closed behind her. She glanced down at the red welts on her ribs where Malcolm's ferocity had increased as he came closer to his climax. She recalled the fingers, almost digging into her, that kept her howling, even as she lurched forward and back against him, despite her unwillingness.

Those weeks of craving had finally culminated in this. Was it worth it? She ran the soap lightly over her body, then stood, basking in the water that cascaded upon her. She itched for more. How long would she wait before she called him? For she certainly wasn't going to see him at *his* beckoning. She'd be the one to do the calling.

Soon she'd have time. The show season had ended for the year, and winter training lightened up as the days bristled with cold. She smiled contentedly, as she reached for her white terrycloth robe and dried part of her hair that had been tapped by the water droplets. Yes, she'd call him. She was in charge now.

"Herbert!" she cried out with pleasure as she heard the voice on the other end of the phone. "Are you back?"

"Last night, late. How have you been?" His deep voice comforted her, as it always had. The protector, her only protector. Otherwise she fended for herself with an assurance she sometimes didn't feel.

"What's up?" She asked, her voice still beaming.

"I think I have a couple buyers for you, for Miss Higgins and that other mare."

"You mean, Miss Higgins' sister, Pennies from Heaven?"

"That's the one."

"Great." Margot smiled. She'd been trying to sell the two mares for a few months, but couldn't get her price. She thought she'd have them over the winter, unable to sell them. But if Herbert thought he'd found a buyer, he probably had.

"A couple I met on one of the islands. I'll bring them up on Saturday, if that's OK."

"Sure. Great," she retorted, weaving the phone wire under and over the fingers of her left hand.

"Say, Margot," Herbert seemed to hesitate. "How did you manage to lose Sally?"

Margot stiffened. "How did you know that?" she said with more ease than she felt. Sally was sabotaging her. Sally was going after Herbert, either as a way to reclaim her old job with Margot, or seduce him into supporting her ventures into this business.

"Ran into her with Rob at the cafe last night, when I got back."

Margot bit her lip in consternation. Why hadn't Herbert called her immediately? Unlike him. What had somehow come between them? He usually called her first, before he did another thing. He often called her before he was back in town so she could greet him, spend that first night with him. What was going on? Had Sally somehow outwitted her, gotten to him first?

She couldn't just breeze over it all as she tried to do with Rob. After all, Herbert was her partner, her backer. If Sally was undermining her before Herbert, she must do something.

Angrily, she told him Sally's demands. "But why do you care?" she asked casually. "You never cared about grooms before."

"I think she has potential."

"Well, yes, she does. But I'm in charge here." Margot bristled, pulling at the cord which rapidly unwound itself from her fingers and snapped across the desk top.

"Quite a girl," he sighed. "Yes, quite a girl." His voice held a sudden, penetrating warmth.

And Margot knew with certainty that he'd been with Sally last night. Somehow she'd arranged it. She'd unexpectedly run across him at the restaurant and maximized her opportunity. When she'd finished dinner with Rob, had she invited herself to Herbert's, leaving Rob to drive home by himself? Or had she waited til she and Rob returned to his farm, and then gone to Herbert's? It didn't matter. What mattered was she'd done it with Herbert. Margot seethed with anger at the treachery. That hussy. That little two-timing bitch.

Margot barely heard Herbert say goodbye and hang up, so busy was she with her own thoughts. She couldn't simply fight fire with fire, for that was Sally's ploy; she was screwing everyone Margot was screwing. Could Margot screw them better? She offered experience—more than Sally's, that was for sure—but maybe youth was more attractive than knowledge.

She squeezed her eyes shut as a knot of fear balled up inside of her. Was Herbert betraying her? She knew, without a second thought, that he was. And what would he do? Would he buy Sally a horse farm? Would he force Margot to sell out to Sally? Or merely force Margot to accept her as an assistant trainer? And where did Sally expect Rob to fit into all of this?

Maybe, now that Herbert was back, he wouldn't fit into it anymore. She probably saw that Herbert was a better bet than Rob.

Margot stamped her foot. She would not have it. She was going to have to strike a deal before she lost everything she had.

CHAPTER 19

She liked being at the barn deep into the night, when the horses barely moved, except with slight rustlings. It was quiet and comforting, almost like a giant cocoon. Now, she reviewed receipts and bills, her brow furrowed in concentration. Her fingers flew at the keys of the computer, when she felt a presence. Not the familiar presence of one of the grooms, but another.

She glanced up, and gasped. For there stood Malcolm, in brown cordoroy pants, a white turtleneck and navy sweater, his gray hair gleaming with health and beauty.

"I came to see you."

She looked up, and smiled absently. "I'm busy."

"I was free," he sat on the edge of the desk.

"Look, Malcolm, how would you like it if I stopped by your office without calling first and demanded that you see me?" Margot tapped her fingers with exasperation. Inwardly, though, she tensed with an exhilarated expectation. He was back!

"I think, knowing you, that I'd accommodate you." Malcolm reached down, sliding his hands under Margot's arms, lifting her til she stood. "I want you," he breathed.

"I don't have time," she stated, gritting her teeth. "I must get these accounts current." But she wondered why she stalled. For, seeing him made her almost pant with desire. But, still, the needed conquest remained. She was to conquer him.

"Everyone has time," he whispered, running his

fingers down her rib cage. She started, a gulp caught in her throat.

"I don't." Margot broke away toward the door. "Now leave. I'll call you in a few days." But she glanced down and saw him hard, beneath his gray suit pants. "Jeez," she tauted, "you must have some imagination if you can get like that already."

He followed, she sidestepped him. But he was quick. He grabbed her arms, pinning her against the wall. "I do," he whispered as his lips found hers.

Then, languidly, he dropped his fingers to her breasts, slowly massaging them through her white cotton turtleneck sweater. She pushed at him, trying to push him away. For this was not what she wanted. She wanted to come to him. She wanted to interrupt him at his work, entice him to her.

She pushed his arms away from the ends of her breasts that already stood, taut with longing. But Malcolm moved his fingers himself. He moved them to her ribs where he lightly began to tickle her.

"Oh no, not again," she breathed, wriggling, trying to free herself. "Cut it out. Now."

But his tickling intensified, til finally, she was engulfed in helpless laughter. He ripped at her shirt, tugged at her bra, nuzzling her breasts, as his fingers flew over her body, wracking her with laughter.

With his knee, he separated her legs, and pressed against her. She grunted, trying halfheartedly to push him away, but too weak and helpless to be effective. He kissed her face, her neck, her shoulders, as his fingers flew across her waist and ribs, holding her in helpless laughter. Gasping for air, she pressed against him, suddenly hot.

"Margot, Margot," he murmured. "I have you at last. I have had only thoughts of you," he breathed, his breath plunging into her ear. She nodded her acquiescence, but she gripped the waist of her jeans making sure he would not pull them down.

His fingers dropped from her breasts to her ribs. "Let go," he commanded softly, but she would not. "Let go." He dug his finger tips into the flesh between her ribs, driving her into gales of helpless laughter, forcing her to relinquish her grip on her jeans. Rapidly he yanked down her jeans and panties, and then, his.

She howled with helplessness, as the fierce fire of desire raced through her. And she knew, with a sort of sorrow, that she had again succumbed to him. No mind, though, for now, all that mattered was to feel him inside of her.

She opened her legs wide, lifting herself to him, and felt him insert himself deep within. She clenched herself rightly around his hips, feeling his throbbing shaft, feeling his mouth on hers, his fingers on her breasts. With a final sigh and heave, she fell back, exhausted. And angry with herself for being so accommodating.

She opened her eyes, peering into his smiling face. "Did you stop by for something?" she asked abruptly, disentangling herself. She hooked a finger onto one of the buttons of his shirt, her finger grazing the hairs on his chest.

"You're so damn cold," he muttered. "Do you ever relax?"

"I'm usually on my guard, looking for snipers." Margot unbuttoned his shirt.

"I'm not one."

"That's what you think," she muttered. "Look, Malcolm, just because I fucked you doesn't mean I trust you." She ran a balled fist across his chest and belly.

He sucked his stomach in.

"The first thing you should understand, Margot," Malcolm looked down at his limp member, "is that I fucked *you*. You had absolutely no intention of having anything to do with me, until I took matters into my own hands."

She looked down, then lifted his member to her hand. "All right," she nodded contritely. She ran her palm across it, then held it firmly. Her other hand began to knead the flesh of his buttocks, drifting into the folds between them.

She glanced down again at his enlarging member, still in her hand. Then she fell to her knees, taking him between her lips, as one hand cupped his scrotom. She felt him begin to sway, felt his hands clasp her head on either side, clutching at her hair. Rapidly, she moved her lips over him, feeling his backside tighten. Just as rapidly, she withdrew, looking up at him with luminous eyes.

"How does it feel?" she breathed, his breath glancing off the tip of his cock.

"Don't stop," he murmured, pushing her head forward.

"Ah, but I must." She backed away, settling back on her heels to gaze at his engorged, throbbing rod.

"How long do you intend to keep Steven's horses? I can sell them for you, if you want."

"Margot," he moaned, stepping toward her, his

member bulging with desire. "Don't stop."

She stood. "Malcolm, I'm afraid not. Not right now. I've got business to attend to. Surely you understand that."

She forced herself to lift her eyes from his startling member. She longed to kiss it til it was spent. She yearned to feel it, wild and wide and strong, inside her again. Instead, she satisfied herself with the amusement of watching it flounder about, as if it were a boat bobbing on the high seas looking for a port.

"Damn you, damn you," he muttered, turning away. She watched his backside flinch, saw his back and shoulders heave, saw him stand absolutely still. At last, he groped for his underwear and pants and put them on.

"I think we'd like to sell High Flyer," he said calmly, turning to face Margot. "We'd like to keep Propriety for awhile til Steven sorts out exactly what he's going to do with the sport."

Margot eyed him quizzically. "Shall I sell High Flyer? Or do you want to?" She dropped her eyes and saw that his member had flattened out.

He stood directly before her. "I think you can do that for us. You work out the asking price." He leaned toward her, bending over her, his breath on her ear again, his lips just millimeters away from her cheek.

Margot swallowed, wondering what was going on. "OK, that's fine," she spoke quickly. "OK, I guess it's time to go."

Suddenly, Malcolm's fingers were on her waist, playing with her skin til she felt the first tickles of laughter. "I just want you to know that I can take you again, and again, and again," he breathed, drumming his fingers on her ribs til she broke into gales of laughter.

And he took her again on the cold leather couch.

Margot had almost sold the mares to Herbert's acquaintances. They'd be back again, this time to ride. And then they'd make a decision. She smiled confidently. It had been a hard sale, but she'd been well-prepared and the horses, well-schooled.

Now Margot leaned against the leather couch, her head against her arms, folded behind her. The barn was silent, for the grooms had just grained, hayed and watered and were off. Only one, Ricky, would be back for the nighttime barn check. She glanced at her watch, then listened to Herbert on the phone.

Did she have time to change before he'd be off the phone and ready to leave with her? Or should they, together, go back to her house, while she changed? Or just forget about changing out of her barn clothes? She'd be in something else soon enough. Her toes and heels jittered in a tiny dance as she waited for him to complete his business call.

At last, he turned toward her, smiling, nodding, as if to announce his imminent availability. She stood, then walked over to perch herself on his knee. No point in not getting started now, she mused, her fingers running over the still hard muscles of his chest under his flannel shirt, gray down vest, and navy parka. For the days were cold now. She leaned her cheek against his, running her fingers over the outline of his eyes, nose, lips, along the profile of his cheek bones and square jaw.

At last he hung up. "Ohh, Margot," he breathed. "I'd forgotten how welcome you are."

She leaned back, arching her back, throwing out her bosom. She felt that familiar tingling, that gentle moistening between her legs. "Now or later, then?" she breathed into his ear, knowing it roused him.

"I'm afraid it can't be either."

"How come?" she cooed, placing her hand on his fly, rubbing the zipper slightly, as if to tease its encased member.

"That's probably not wise," he subtly pushed her back, as if to ease her off his lap.

"How come?" She was suddenly alert, smelling, feeling, tasting danger.

"I am having—" he said it slowly deliberately, as if he were trying to determine what exactly he should say to her.

"Sally. A date with Sally!" Margot exploded.

"Actually, yes. How did you know?" He seemed relieved.

If he is relieved, she thought, then he must be anxious about me knowing.

"Did she promise to screw you if you gave her a horse farm?" Margot leaned forward, her mouth almost touching his as she whispered her venom. "Does a blow job buy her an assistant trainer position? What about a hand job? She just gets her old job back as groom? Which one is it?" Margot sneared, grinding her hips into Herbert, hoping to see him squirm under the interrogation.

"It was good enough for you," he said evenly. "Now if you'll excuse me."

"Which is it?" She screamed, hurtling herself off

179

him. "Which one? You owe me that."

"I owe you clients, financial backing and friendship, Margot," he said coldly.

She stared back. "You think by screwing her you're giving me friendship?" Her voice was high, derisive. "Because the next thing I know, you'll ask me to leave the premises so she can take over!" Margot screeched.

He aroused all her old terrors and uncertainties about him and her business. She'd thought he was unequivocally devoted to her. But no longer. Icy fear twisted around her limbs.

"Who I spend my evenings with is, I believe, my business. That's why I no longer have a wife."

Margot swallowed, ashamed at her prying, horrified by his independence. "You can't do this," she wailed, clasping her hands together imploringly.

"What is the matter with you, Margot?" Herbert laughed shortly. But then his blue eyes hardened.

She shook her head. It was more than Sally usurping her position with Herbert. She knew, somehow, she could fight her off successfully. Instead, it was Sally's flaunting her power over Margot. Sally was attacking her through Margot's men. First there was Pete, then Rob, and now the staunchest of supporters, Herbert.

Margot was no longer invincible.

And there was more.

Sally gave herself to everyone, and not Margot. Tears blotted her vision. It was then she realized the worst of her unhappiness. Sally would never come to her, or be hers. Now that she had found Herbert, she would see that she didn't need Margot to give her anything. Herbert could do it all. That was the message she was giving to Margot.

Margot shook her head from side to side. There was nothing she could give Sally anymore. She had lost Sally. And yet, she wondered how much longer she could bear the tortures of longing, and not having, the woman.

"What does she want you for?" She asked miserably.

"Ahh, Margot," Herbert said soothingly, laying her head on his shoulder. "Jealous, aren't you?"

She didn't move, giving no sign that she had heard. "Afraid, aren't you?"

Still, she gave no sign of hearing him.

"Malcolm Forsythe shook you up too, didn't he?" Herbert patted her head fondly. "Ah, Margot. There *is* a chink in your wall, after all, isn't there?" He said softly, turning her head so he could kiss her cheek.

She burrowed against him, feeling the bristles of his beard against her cheek. She pressed harder, willing his strong, secure spirit into her woebegone one.

"I won't desert you, Margot. I won't force you into anything you don't want," he whispered kissing the lobes of her ears. "I promise you. Don't forget, this is still business for me. This is sill an investment. I'm not one to throw money around." He laid his large, pawlike hand on her breast, softly massaging it. He pressed his palms against her nipples til Margot felt the faint nibblings of desire.

She lay against him, feeling the swelling within her. He felt so comfortable. His words were so comforting. This was the first port in the recent storm she had found. She felt his fingers dip to her waist and raise her wool turtleneck, so that he could feel the flesh of her stomach and her breasts.

She didn't move, knowing that without doing anything, she was seducing him and once again cementing their relationship. Tonight, no matter what his rush to meet Sally was, it would be Sally who got sloppy seconds.

Margot still lay absolutely still, listening to his breathing quicken, even as she felt her own heart hammer. She felt him tug at her jeans, unfastening the button, struggling with her fly. Then his fingers dipped down to her crotch, nestling in its contours of loveliness. He pushed her legs wider with his paws, and nuzzled her further with his fingers.

The longed for moisture gathered between her legs. She glanced down and saw his turgid member pulling at the closures of his flannel pants. But she waited, knowing that he had rebuffed her earlier. She would wait for him to ask her.

At last, his breath heaving in rapid little bursts, he lifted her hand off her leg and placed it on his zipper. "Margot," he whispered. "I erred before. I made a mistake when I told you I was in a rush."

Margot smiled, a glint of happiness and relief in her eyes. "Are you sure?" she rubbed him slowly as he nodded his assurance.

She slithered sideways so that now she faced him. Adroitly, she removed his hard cock from his pants, fondling it with delicate touches. Then, hiking herself up, as he played with her breasts and she ran her fingers over his stomach, she placed herself firmly on his rod.

The heat seared her, sending shivers throughout

her body. She pressed upon him, tightening her muscles vigorously. He grunted his pleasure, closed his eyes, and pressed her down on him harder til they came in mutual desire.

"I promise you," Herbert leaned forward, burying his face between her breasts, "you will not be abandoned." He pressed them against his cheeks. His tongue wagged from side to side, touching them.

"Thank you," she whispered. She looked down at his sword, starting to stiffen again. With the sudden energy of one whose sentence has been reprieved, she jumped off his lap onto all fours on the floor of her office, waiting. Herbert scrambled after her, taking her from behind with deep satisfying thrusts of understanding and commitment.

CHAPTER 20

Margot floundered. Too many horses to train, too many stalls to clean, too many horses to grain, too much administration to administer. Here it was, in the middle of January, a five-degree day, and I'm working harder than ever. What will I do this summer?

Nervously, she tapped her nails on the kitchen table, account records spread before her. She'd been up too late last night working the horses. In the past, it had always seemed to ease off at this time of year. It just hadn't seemed so relentless.

She sipped her coffee. First, she'd hire a secretary.

Second, she'd hire an—she balked at the thought. She needed an assistant. Not a groom to lunge or long-line the horses, but an assistant trainer. The thought had been niggling at her for weeks. Sally. She would offer Sally a job.

She knew from Herbert that Sally was still at Rob's, that she was still a groom, that she still balled him. She knew, too, that she'd only balled Herbert once. He hadn't let her do it again. She took another gulp of coffee. It was time to call her, invite her over. It wouldn't, of course, be a free and clear offer. It would have the same strings attached as before.

For Margot craved Sally as much as ever. No matter how she spent her time with Ed or Herbert or her grooms, she yearned for Sally. She yearned for Sally as she yearned for Malcolm. He hadn't been around either.

"Coffee?" Margot held a red mug out to her guest, but Sally shook her head. She stood in Margot's kitchen, on the opposite side of the round oak table, her feet spread two feet apart, her arms akimbo.

"How's your job?" Margot asked. She held her voice aloof.

"Fine."

"Are you an assistant trainer yet?"

"Nope." Sally's eyes narrowed. "But you know that. So why did you invite me over? To gloat that things were no better there than here? That no matter how much I fuck my brains out with Rob I still get to be a groom?" Sally glared at Margot.

"If you fucked your brains out with me, you'd get to be an assistant trainer," Margot said harshly, clutching the hot mug in both her hands, steadying her trembling body.

Sally's mouth dropped open. "What do you mean?" she asked warily.

"I need an assistant trainer."

"So, hire one."

"I want you to be my assistant trainer. Remember, I saw you work that horse, Tad."

"Thad," Sally corrected, pulling out a chair to sit down. "So, hire me."

"I'm trying to."

"Well, what's the problem?"

The women faced each other, as if they were in opposite corners of the ring, squaring off. Their voices were brittle, hard, each one jockeying for a better position.

"Negotiations," Margot retorted. She placed her cup on the counter and headed through her dining room, filled with a large oak table and six chairs and a large breakfront with her china dishes, to the flowered living room. "Come here."

She settled herself on the couch, stretching her legs out, and turned her head to face her fire, bristling with the sounds of crackling wood.

Sally entered the room. "Seems to me, Margot, that if you want me that badly, I hold all the cards. I don't have to fuck one single brain of mine out," she said icily. "Unless," she paused, "I want to." She stood, leaning against the door frame, staring at Margot.

Margot's eyes searched hers, then dropped to the thin waist in the black leather belt, the slim but curved hips, the long and limber legs. "Noo," she said slowly, "I guess you're right. I probably should

185

have waited for you to come begging for a job here."
She forced herself to turn back toward the fire.

She could imagine Sally's curly head lapping up
the remnants of Rob's nightly lust. She could see her
fingers kneading his tight, muscular buttocks. She
could see Sally bent over on all fours, Rob above her
rocking her breasts to and fro with his powerfully
long hands. "But that's not my style," she said. "I
have a job offer. I'll give it to the best person."

There, she heaved a sigh. The card. There'd be a
competition.

"How do you determine that?" Sally asked icily,
sitting on the edge of the couch near Margot's feet.

"Unfortunately, there are different criteria." Now
Margot turned to look Sally full in the face. Her eyes
drifted to Sally's breasts.

Sally returned the look, then shifted her focus to
the fire. Slowly, she raised both of her hands to her
breasts. In circling motions, she rubbed them evenly
and languidly, as if she had nothing in the world to
do that Sunday afternoon.

Margot could only stare in fascination. Despite
herself, she bent her legs upward, pressing her buttocks into the couch for a firmer foundation.

Then Sally pulled her heavy knit sweater over her
head, exposing her bare skin, her lovely saucy breasts
with their pert nipples upended. Again, she placed
her hands on her breasts, moving them in slow,
undulating motion.

Margot's breath quickened. Would Sally be hers at
last? Or was she merely teasing her again, so that
Margot would be *forced* to beg Sally to take the job.
Unknowingly, Margot dropped her fingers to her

crotch and lightly fingered the fabric covering her yearning, tingling cavity.

Sally glanced down, a knowing smile suddenly dancing on her lips. She unfastened her own jeans and stood, pushing them and her panties to the rag rug. Now, she was naked before Margot.

Margot squirmed. It was so blissful with the crackling fire, the white, wintery day outside, and this woman who at last might be hers. But she didn't move. For surely, Sally had something in mind and Margot did not want to disturb her mating call.

Sally leaned back against the couch, her backside resting against Margot's toes, now curled in anticipation. Sally dropped her fingers to her crotch, as her other hand caressed her breasts. Margot's body tingled rapturously. Could she bear it any longer? Would she be forced to bolt upright and take Sally herself?

Hypnotized, she watched Sally frig herself with increasing abandon and absorption: her eyes closed, her breath in quick gasps, her hips arching frantically as she sought release. Margot pressed her own palm against her crotch, swaying her hips against it. Is that what she wanted this first time? Her own finger? No, she'd wait for Sally. but first she'd watch her.

Her own breath heaved, as she saw Sally pulsate against her finger, saw her fingers pull and tweak her breasts, and finally, in one shuddering breath, she saw Sally fall back, relieved and released.

Margot moved against her hand, visualizing the girl at her peak of ecstasy. But then she stopped. She would not have it that way. Sally would do it to her herself.

"That was a nice show, Sally," she said coldly. It might as well have been a dancing and singing act, or at the very most a peep show.

Sally sat up, smiling. "Did you like it?"

"Are those your credentials?" Margot asked icily, at last able to uncurl her toes.

"You've just read the beginning of my resume, Margot." Sally stood and walked over to Margot's head. She bent down, her breasts falling against Margot's, and kissed her hard on the lips.

Margot gasped and opened her mouth to receive the longed-for, hoped-for tongue. She sat up, reaching for Sally's breasts, and Sally ran her hands under Margot's red sweater for hers. Rampant lust raced through Margot, as she pulled Sally more tightly toward her in a frenzy.

Only the ringing of the telephone roused them from the frenetic feeling and grasping as they fondled each other's breasts and kissed each other's lips and cheeks and necks.

"I won't answer," Margot breathed. For the answering machine would receive the message. Still, even as she basked in the feel of Sally's hands upon her and hers upon Sally, she half-listened to her voice asking the caller to leave a message.

Suddenly, she stopped. For it was Malcolm. At long last. How ironic, she thought. Just when I'm in the middle of one of the two things I have craved. He, of course, was the other.

"Oh, wait, Sally, I should get that." She bolted upright, and stretched for the phone just as he seemed to be ending his message.

"Hello?" She said breathlessly. Don't let him have hung up. She leaned across the sofa arm, pulling the wire cord toward her.

"Ah, Margot, I was afraid you weren't there," he said in his deep, sonorous voice.

"But I am."

Sally leaned over Margot, reaching for her breasts, tweaking their ends. Margot turned to her back, fully exposing herself to Sally. Now Sally reached for the button and the zipper of Margot's jeans, and swiftly loosened them. Margot lurched upright at her feel.

"Are you free tonight?" He inquired brusquely as if setting up an appointment.

"Um," she hesitated. "When? In how many hours?" Would she and Sally have finished their business? Sally buried her face in Margot's stomach, then covered her with kisses, as her other hand reached for Margot's mound. Margot arched upward, grunting.

"Excuse me?" Malcolm said.

"I—uh—" Sally placed her tongue inside Margot. "Wanted to know what time you were thinking—uh—about." Voluptuous excitement cascaded through her as Sally licked her moist cavity.

"7:30. It's 3:30 now."

Four hours. Would they be done? Probably. They'd shower, have coffee, sit around talking. Yes, she'd be done. Sally spread Margot's legs and dove between them, so that only her forehead seemed to peer out from between.

"Oh, God," Margot moaned as Sally's tongue flicked over her throbbing knob of desire.

"Excuse me?" Malcolm's voice carried irritation.

189

"Ohh," she breathed deeply, "yesss, yes I am," she gasped, reached for Sally's head, and pushed it down upon her further.

"Perhaps the Italian place?"

"Uh—uh," Margot replied vaguely. Usually he was so preemptory. Why not tonight?

Sally scooted around, placing her mouth near Margot's mouth. Margot reached out, hungering for it.

"I didn't catch that." Malcolm sounded annoyed. He wasn't one to play second fiddle.

"Anything," she gasped, plunging her tongue into Sally, sweeping her hands across her thighs and knees and calves. "Anything," she repeated, her voice lurching unsteadily. "I'll see you at 7:30."

"Very well, then," he replied crossly.

Margot heard the line go dead, as she gripped the receiver in the throes of passion. Even as their tongues plunged into one another and their hands fumbled with each other's breasts and bellies, Margot unknowingly gripped the receiver to her.

At last, Sally. Sally, at last, clung and whispered to her, nestled and nuzzled her, her bottom saucily swaying with her hips, her pert breasts heaving with exertion, her hair wild with the distractions. Margot ran her hands over the girl, still not believing that after all this time, she held her. Would it have been so glorious, she wondered, if she'd acquiesced to her so many months ago?

Who knew? She shrugged, ripples of sensuality flooding through her until she climaxed with passionate moans of ecstasy. To Margot, it was the culmination of months of daydreaming and imaginings.

But to Sally, it was clearly all business.

"So, when do I start?" She smiled earnestly, like a school girl eagerly waiting for a grade on a report. The shower water pelted them as they stood side by side.

Margot froze. Was that all there was to it, then? "Two weeks. You need to give Rob two weeks notice." She remembered kicking Sally out the moment she had resigned months ago. "Unless of course, he kicks you out first. Then come on over."

Sally nodded as she lathered her body.

Margot eyed her, still drinking in her beauty. "Sally," she said a bit harshly. "The deal doesn't end now, you know, don't you?"

"I know. I know what the job entails." Sally poured green shampoo onto her hands and rubbed them into her red hair.

Margot winced, hoping that Sally would not have viewed this as a business arrangement. She had hoped that once Sally was with her, she would have changed her view of Margot and wanted her as desperately as she was wanted.

"Just wanted no misunderstandings." But somehow the thrill had palled. Margot replaced the small rectangular soap bar in its holder and looked at Sally quizzically. "It's all business to you, isn't it? Everyone is just another way to get up one more rung on the ladder, isn't it?"

Sally turned her head and nodded. "Yes, yes it is. Quite simply. I'm fucking my way to the top."

"You like it, at least, don't you?" Margot always had, even when she worked her hardest fucking the most repulsive of men. She threw her head back, letting the water pound onto her face.

"No."

Abruptly, Margot stepped back, scanning the girl. "What?" she screeched.

"No, not at all."

"*Never?*"

"Never."

"Even when you come?"

"I don't come," Sally replied simply, letting the shower water beat the soap out of her hair.

"You *don't?* What happens?"

"I pretend. I just fuck to get what I need. Maybe it secures my job with Rob, maybe it gets me a better job with you. Maybe Pete or Corey or Craig cut me a break on the barn check one night." She shrugged. "Any number of things." She was so matter-of-fact that Margot could only stare in shock.

"And with that girl Eva at Rob's?"

Again, Sally shrugged, as if to say, it was all nothing.

Margot gritted her teeth. "And me?" She tried to say it casually, but she feared the answer. She too was just another notch on the belt. There was not one scintilla of desire.

Again, Sally shrugged. "Sorry, Margot. But you asked. No one has ever asked before." She turned toward the faucets. "I'll turn them off if you're done."

They were silent. Disappointment hung heavily in the air for Margot. For Sally, resignation hung there. Margot kept glancing at the girl in wonder, imagining what it would be like never to love it, never to come, never to relish one more hump. It seemed

rather pointless, then, she decided, to sidle up
behind Sally and take her. Sally would, of course,
oblige. But that just wouldn't be enough for Margot.

CHAPTER 21

Margot sighed, feeling the winter doldrums settling
upon her. They always came upon her in the dark,
cold days of February when it seemed that there
would be no end to winter. The relentless struggle of
fighting the cold and the ice and the snow.

This year was particularly lonely. Ed had bid
adieu just a few nights ago. He'd be moving to Cali-
fornia for several months to file a special report.
She'd miss that swashbuckling manner of his, as he
wielded his straps and sticks til he stuck out hard and
far and took her roughly. Funny, how they'd never
done it any other way. No tenderness for him.

And Herbert. Gone to the Swiss Alps for winter
skiing. She missed that reliable body and easy
humor.

And Malcolm. Gone, it would seem, forever. Their
last meeting had held so much insinuated promise.
There would be more. And then there wasn't. He
had returned to the bustling streets of New York, the
zooming traffic and the exotic lunches. Margot
couldn't determine why this had happened, unless he
had given up with her, decided she really wasn't that
enticing after all. She had last heard from him weeks
ago.

So the days and weeks loomed long.

For she was left with the regular boys and Sally. And somehow Sally had lost that glow. She felt as if she manhandled Sally, knowing that she only play-acted. Her gasps were fakes, her cries were fraudulent, her undulations were hypocritical. Margot still sought that pert body and delighted in feeling the curves and silky skin, but she had lost that same passionate, obsessive longing.

It wasn't as if she didn't think of her. For she did. Virtually all the time, trying to determine what would make Sally hot. What would make her crave Margot's body? For unless she craved Margot, she would never be hers totally. Margot would not be in control.

"Enough," Margot said aloud, slamming the black leather cover of the record book closed. She stood and stretched, ready to return to the farmhouse. As she strode down the barn aisle, the horses nickered or scuffed the sides of the stalls. Margot kicked at stray strands of hay.

Once outside, she breathed deeply, glad to shake off the wrap of record-keeping books. In the distance, she spied Sally, just leaving the lower barn.

"Sally!" She called out, her voice echoing in the silent, black night.

Sally stopped, turning toward Margot's voice. "Hi."

Margot caught up. "Wanna come for hot chocolate?" She turned the collar up and buried her head within its warmth.

"Oh, yeah," Sally answered, her voice muffled by a scarf tied around her head and neck. "Sounds good.

I'm frozen."

"I should've driven," Margot muttered, her feet crackling on the glazed snow that covered the ground. She clapped her hands together.

"Nah, you would've spent ten minutes warming your car up," Sally laughed. She grabbed Margot's elbow as she slipped on a patch of ice. Even through her down jacket, Margot tensed at her touch, but said nothing more.

Once inside the warm farmhouse, they carelessly hung their coats on the brass coat hanger by the door. Remnants of the fire lay on the bottom of the fireplace.

"You make the fire, Margot," Sally suggested, peeling off her winter clothing. "I'll do the chocolate. I can't ever get fires to burn. Once the paper has burned up, the fire dies out too," Sally winked cheerfully.

"I'm not so good at the hot chocolate, so we probably have a decent deal," Margot retorted good-naturedly, throwing her sweater on top of her jacket. "The packets are in the cabinet to the left of the stove. And . . ."

"And the water's in the sink," Sally giggled, swatting Margot tenderly on her behind.

Margot breathed sharply, then turned to enter the still-warm living room. Embers glistened in the hearth, as she prodded the fire with the metal rod. She lay a few thin branches and crumbled some additional newspapers. The warmth of the sudden blaze relaxed her. She sat down cross-legged, still prodding and poking the ashes to ignite some of the wood.

She'd take Sally tonight, of course. Sally knew that. She was so pleasantly acquiescent, always prepared to have it done to her when in truth she had no satisfaction. Margot recognized the signs now. She could see how quickly Sally recuperated from their fondling, how short-lived her heaving breaths were, how dry her body was.

Why? She wondered, replacing the metal prodder in its brass holder next to a shovel and broom that she'd never so much as touched. Why didn't Sally get it off with Margot or even herself? She'd told Margot, as they lay strewn across Margot's double bed that she rarely got herself off alone. Then Margot, fascinated, had asked to watch.

Sure enough, though Sally tantalizingly fondled her breasts and her mound, though she arched and groaned convulsively as if to convince her body to let go, she was not able to find that release. She fell back among the four white pillows, tired, but unfulfilled. She shrugged, as if to apologize. "It's always been like that," she simply said.

Now Margot pondered it, wondering if Sally would never come. And if Sally never came, she would be bereft of a wondrous thrill. But more importantly, she would never be Margot's. She would never have the feeling of being beholden unto her, of beseeching her for more fiery caresses, steamy kisses and frenzied hands. She'd never feel the entanglement toward Margot that the others felt.

"Umm, it smells great," Sally mumbled, carefully placing the green wooden tray on the oak coffee table. She settled back on the couch, lifting a mug in her hands. Margot reached backward, her brow still furrowed in concentration.

Funny, she mused silently, as she cupped the mug between her palms, I thought it would be enough just to have her, but I see that half the fun of having people is seeing how much they want you. Herbert, even Malcolm, Ed! Like a bolt, she knew.

Why, it was Ed who couldn't get it up unless he'd beat or been beaten! Ed, who could be coddled and licked to no avail. Is Sally like Ed? Margot looked at her inquiringly in the startling realization. She was appalled. For Sally was her perky little plaything, not something to be wallopped and bludgeoned. Could it be?

Excitedly, she stood, replacing her mug. "Sally, I have an idea," she whispered. "Take off your clothes."

"OK," Sally nodded willingly, as she always did.

She kept her part of the deal. In return for her title, she always obliged Margot. She'd bend down in the front seat of the jeep and lick Margot as she drove the bumpy roads. She'd finger her while Margot oiled a saddle. She'd let Margot lustfully fondle her breasts as she prepared coffee in the office in the early morning hours.

Now Sally stood naked before Margot. Margot felt her own loins tingle with anticipation. The sight of Sally's nakedness aroused her, shortened her breath, moistened her.

"Sally," Margot said softly, "bend over the arm of the couch, with your butt in the air. That's right." Margot took a deep, cleansing breath as she gazed at the ovals before her, luscious like spring peaches.

Sally's breasts dangled onto the couch seat as she

held onto the arm. "Why?"

"Just wait," Margot whispered. She raised her arm and swiftly brought it down on Sally's backside, once, then twice.

Sally howled in surprise and then pain. "Margot?" Her voice was sharply inquisitive, but she didn't move.

Again, Margot raised her hand, bringing it down hard and firm on Sally's buttocks. "Stop!" Sally gasped, bringing her hand to cover her backside. "Stop! Please!" She wailed, her buttocks twisting from side to side.

"Move your hand," Margot said huskily, as the happy moisture gathered between her legs. Obediently, Sally brought it to the pillows, clenching it tightly. Again, she brought her hand down, creating red streaks of lust. Sally cried out, but she didn't move. She wriggled, but she didn't stand.

Margot pressed her own legs together to staunch the lust that flowed through her. Her own chest heaved with arousal.

"Stop, Margot, stop," Sally screeched, her hips arching and swaying under Margot's repeated slaps. "Oh, lord, oh lord," she cried out, gasping for breath, writhing in anguish. "Ohh, Margot," she wailed, "Don't stop, don't, just don't!"

Spasmodically, Sally wagged her buttocks to and fro against the couch as the slaps rained down upon them. With a huge cry of astonished arousal, she grasped the couch pillows with all her might, flung her legs wide, begging for more, until her screams of despair culminated in a scream of utter, voluptuous satisfaction.

A sly smile crossed Margot's face. She fell across Sally's back, pumping against her until she, too, came with joyful abandon.

They lay entangled in each other's arms until slowly Margot pulled herself off and sank to the rug. She smiled with amusement and satisfaction. Finally, after the months of repeated fingers and caresses and kisses, she had pleasured Sally with the flat of her hand.

Sally sank to the floor beside Margot, her chest still heaving. "Margot," she whispered, wide-eyed with surprise. "I did it. I finally did it."

Margot nodded, patting Sally's bent knee.

"How did you know?" She breathed.

"Experience, I guess." She shrugged, masking her glee. Sally had, for the moment, been hers. She had belonged to her for the first time. "What did you think?"

"I think I owe you a lot. You are heaven-sent," she whispered, turning to kiss Margot full in the lips, her tongue playing with Margot's, her fingers drifting across the tips of Margot's breasts til her nipples again stood taut and hard.

"What do you think you owe me?" Margot asked, caressing Sally's satiated, lovely body. Her shoulders curved delicately, her waist nipped in suggestively.

Sally's fingers dropped to Margot's crotch and played with the folds, til Margot was hot with renewed longing. She reached out for Sally's buttocks again, taking a bit of skin between her forefinger and thumb. Sally jerked in surprise, but did not stop her gentle massage of Margot. Margot took more folds of skin, pinching, pressing, hoping that little flecks of pain would unhinge Sally again, would show her that she truly owed everything to Margot.

Sally squealed, pushing closer. She lay Margot back on the rug, pressing her vulva against Margot's, her fingers wagging deep within. Margot pinched and pulled at Sally til each felt the other begin to press harder and faster, yearning for release together, for the first time.

For a second time, Sally squealed, as the passion tore through her body. For a second time, Margot came with a satisfied release, buoyed by the knowledge that she had at least succeeded.

Sally fell upon Margot's breast. "Margot," she whispered, lifting her head. "I—I really thank you."

"Good," Margot answered noncommittantly. Sudden fear shot through her that Sally would realize that now that she was able to find pleasure, that she was not frigid, that she would again leave Margot and seek greener pastures. She ran her hands over the fiery red of Sally's behind.

"I owe you, Margot."

"What do you owe me?"

"Complete, undying loyalty."

Margot smiled with satisfaction. Coming from Sally, that wasn't bad.

CHAPTER 22

It was a gamble. And so far it was paying off. Steven Forsythe had dropped her off in front of the enormous white granite office building on Madison Avenue in New York City so she could say hello to his father.

Steven had called earlier to say he'd stop by one vacation day from college. They rode together as friends, no longer teacher and student. And then when he mentioned that he'd be driving to the city the following day, she suddenly, even surprising herself, asked to accompany him.

But it was only as they neared the city, along the FDR Drive when Steven asked where he should drop her off, that Margot casually mentioned she just might stop by and see his father if he weren't out of town. They had some things to square up. Purposely, she insinuated that he owed her money.

No, Steven retorted, he wasn't out of town. But often his father would be tied up for hours at a time, and she might want to call him first. But Margot reassured him. She could always saunter around Saks Fifth Avenue. Perhaps the new style for horseback-riding clothes would be appropriate for her.

Now Margot sat primly in a straight-backed leather chair. He was in, but he was in a meeting. Margot unfolded the newspaper and waited. No matter how long she waited, it was still her decision.

But she didn't need to wait long. She sensed a presence in front. As she slowly raised her eyes from the paper in front of her, traveling past shiny black leather laced-up shoes, the cuffed pants of a gray pinstripe suit, a white shirt and red tie, he felt her heart hammer. She looked up, her eyes growing wide at the sight of his handsome, rugged face and his steel gray hair.

He held out a hand. "Margot, what a pleasure," he seemed to gush.

"Just in the neighborhood. Thought I'd stop by," she grinned broadly at the preposterousness of such a comment.

"Let me welcome you. I've got a couple phone calls to attend to, but why don't you come back to my office?" He took her elbow, guiding her through long wide corridors to an office in a far corner.

Margot stopped stock still. "I like to pretend I've been around, but I've *never* seen an office this big before. It's as big as five of the show stalls." Margot swung around. "Though, of course, the horses don't have floor to ceiling windows on three sides," she giggled.

"Maybe they should," Malcolm answered dryly, picking up the telephone receiver. "Ah, yes, Gloria, we need to restructure that company. We need to have serious discussions about that. Now? Of course." Malcolm settled into his large swivel chair and raised his legs to the mahogany desk.

Margot crossed her arms with ill-concealed anticipation. It was all so new. She wandered about the room, tentatively feeling the gray textured wallpaper and the gray and maroon chairs. She glanced at Malcolm chatting comfortably and confidently at his desk, and tilted her head with an amused smile, wondering what he thought of her visit.

Had he merely dismissed her these past weeks? Had he always dismissed her, thinking she was just a toy for his weekends in the country? He glanced up at her, smiling, beckoning her closer. Margot was confused. The confidence she'd felt as she clicked her heels across the marble lobby floors was dissipating in his powerful presence. And yet, he never lost his dignity in her world of horses. He carried it wherever he went.

Margot walked over, and in a sudden rush, bent down and gently bit his ear lobe. She saw him start, then beam, then blush. She bent down, nuzzling his neck, thrusting her tongue into the recesses of his ear. He talked on.

With a sudden sense of purpose, Margot lifted his tie, tossing it over his shoulder, and began to unbutton his button at his navel. Quickly, he retrieved his tie, patting it down, a stern warning on his face. But Margot managed to stick two fingers into his shirt. She rubbed his stomach, entwining her fingers among the hairs.

"Do you like to be tickled?" she whispered as her fingers wandered to his rib cage.

Malcolm shook his head vigorously, but Margot ran her strong fingers over his ribs, jolting him. She ran her tongue over her lips enticingly, as she unbuttoned still another, then another. Malcolm's eyes narrowed, as he tried to straighten his shirt in his pants, but Margot pulled at it, pulling the shirt tales out. Now, she placed both hands on his stomach, running them over his ribs and chest. She saw his awkward heaves, a controlled guffaw.

"Gloria, why don't we continue this tomorrow? I'll

meet you at 7:30? Breakfast at the Regency? Fine."
Malcolm slammed the phone down. "*This* is my
office."

"I know that," Margot said contritely.

"I don't expect to have this happen in my office."
He struggled to remove her hands, so she dropped
her mouth to his stomach, pecking at it with his lips.
He lurched upward, stifling a gulp of laughter.

"It happened in mine," she said demurely. Margot
slipped to the floor, folding her legs behind her and
placed her hand on his zipper. She could barely feel
him through the wool of his suit.

"That is different."

"Why?" She rubbed him lightly, but he did not
respond. "That's where I earn my money, just as you
earn yours here."

Malcolm pulled his legs off the desk and stumbled
to his feet, throwing Margot backwards. "I think this
is not the place."

"I didn't come begging," she retorted, smiling. "I
came to tease you. I thought it would be fun." She
stood and walked toward a wall of windows. "You
hadn't called me. I thought it was time to call you,
see what you were doing." She raised her hands to
her head, releasing the mountain of hair piled.

"You're lovely," Malcolm said softly, stroking his
chin and regarding her closely. "But disruptive."

Margot winked and then strolled about the room.
She dropped her suede jacket to the chair by the
door. She removed her shoes near the chair by the
coffee table. She lifted one leg to the table and carefully removed one black stocking, then the other,
flinging them overhead as she did so.

She swiveled slowly, her delight growing as his consternation grew. "Now what?" She shrugged.

"I have calls, Margot. I don't know what."

"Surely a man of your calibre can control his phone calls." With a deliberately casual movement, she walked over to him and planted a full kiss on his lips, pressing her breasts against his chest, urging her hips against his. Smothering a groan, he stepped back, but Margot had inserted a finger in the waist of his pants.

His head spun as the intercom buzzed. "I must get that," he muttered. As he turned, Margot slipped her hand to his member, no longer as insipidly soft as it had been.

"Yes? Put him through." Malcolm sat on the edge of his desk, one knee bent. Margot moved toward him and placed her hand on his crotch again. He took a deep unsteady breath. "Ah, good day, Sir William." He raised his voice slightly. "I wanted to be sure that you were pleased with the arrangements of the sale."

Margot sidled up to Malcolm, cupping his ear in her hands.

"What makes you think you can disrupt my life? What makes you think you can stand in the middle of the arena when I give a lesson?" She whispered.

Malcolm shook his head, shooing her away. "Yes, we priced it at $84 a share for a total of $564 million."

"Why can you just race in and pull your kid out, disrupting his life and mine?" Her sibilant whisper seemed to echo through the room.

"Yes, all the voting rights." He pushed her away.

But as he stretched his hand out, Margot grabbed it and placed it on her breast, her own hand on top of his. She forced him to touch her. Angrily, he clamped his hand over the receiver. "Please leave me alone."

"Why is it all right to tickle me til I give in to you?" She leaned forward whispering, but not releasing his hand on her breast. "Why do you demand I be at my house at 7:00 and throw a tantrum if I am not?" Margot's breast heaved in anger. For the more she thought about his rude, unruly behavior, the more irritated she became.

Quickly, before he could grab hold of her, she hoisted down his zipper and reached within its confines to remove his prick, startling large for a man in the midst of a business conversation.

"Sixty percent?" His voice quavered as Margot took him between her lips. He pushed her head away from him, but Margot slid her hand beneath him to cup his scrotum in her hands. "I think that's—uhg—" he grunted as she nibbled at the end of his prick, "—excessive."

Malcolm shut his eyes, as Margot fondled him. "Sir William, why don't we consider this tonight, and give you a ring tomorrow?" He hesitated. "Yes, of course, if you wish to have a conference call now, I can arrange that." He rolled his eyes heavenward, then reached behind to press his intercom.

"Can you reach Worthington, set up a conference call?" He grunted as Margot took him full in the mouth, till all but the hilt was hidden in the deep recesses of her mouth. "This is enough," his voice radiated anger. "I have a deal that's about to

206

blow—"

"And I'm blowing you. What a coincidence," she tittered. Then, deftly, Margot lifted off her black and white wool dress, pulled down her white silk bikinis and kneeled before him in a black garter belt and small lacy brassiere that delicately cupped her breasts. She swiveled forward, her lithe body ready to tantalize him.

"Margot," he hissed. But suddenly, as she delicately handled his sword, his face contorted, he gripped her breast, and tensed his body.

She pulled back. She had not finished tantalizing him yet. Laughingly, she settled on her haunches, watching him strain to control himself. "Let 'er rip," she suggested artfully.

"Not there? Fine." He spoke into the intercom, then returned to the telephone. "Sir William, I'm afraid Worthington is not in. I'll keep on top of it, and phone you just as soon as I hear something. You're six hours ahead, aren't you?"

Margot stood, pressing her near-naked body against his, rubbing her breasts against his chest, her quim against his throbbing prick.

"Sir William, what would you say to fifty-one percent voting rights? I think I could manage that." He hurled Margot away again with his foot. But she returned, leaning over the desk so that her breasts dangled beside him, just touching the desktop. His voice quavered as he bid farewell. He slammed the phone down and stood. "Damn it, that's unprofessional and rude."

"So are you," she retorted. "And talk about professional. Look at you: you're hanging out ten miles."

Malcolm looked down and smirked sheepishly. "And now what do you expect me to do? How do you expect me to conduct business this way?" With difficulty, he stuffed his cock back in his pants.

"Maybe I don't expect it. You didn't seem to mind barging into my life. What's the difference?" She asked sweetly, sitting on the desk top. She raised her legs, bent her knees and dropped her fingers to her crotch, delicately touching herself.

She sure hoped he'd locked the door, she half-heartedly thought. She sure hoped his three walls of windows were high enough above all the other windows of New York that no one could see her exposed this way. She glanced at Malcolm. His cock throbbed within his wool pants.

"Want to call a truce?" She smiled and held out a hand, as the other dangled and fiddled with her cunt.

He said nothing. Instead he walked across the room, looked her in the eyes, bent and kissed her lips, and placed his hand over hers at the entrance to her body. "How do you spend your time when I'm not there? What do you do for laughs?" He reached for his member, removing it once again, and lifted it to the entrance of her cavity, just touching its curves.

Margot looked away for a moment, picturing Sally. Picturing herself and Sally. How they fell upon each other in the tackroom, brandishing leather reins or nylon whips; or the bedroom, using bathrobe ties and the flat of their hands, or the fireplace, where they'd take the night off and just loll about caressing, kissing, lapping at each other for seemingly endless hours. She relished Sally's squeals of ecstasy, just as she relished the feel of her saucy body to her touch.

But that would be at the farm, upstate. Now, she had Malcolm, who stood patiently waiting for her, his prick like a dog lapping at the water's edge.

"What do you want, Malcolm?" Margot breathed, reaching for his shoulders with one hand. With the other, she pulled his cock closer, and arched forward so that she half-sat on the desk.

"You," he replied, his voice husky. He bent his head forward, burying it between her lush breasts and tried to enter her. But she backed off.

"I don't know, Malcolm," she whispered her reply. Even so, she reached out, pulling his cock closer to her, gripping his ass in her firm fingers. Now, she slid forward again so that he just touched her quim.

"Damn, Margot," he groaned, as she pressed toward him. She saw the trickling beginnings of his lust. "Come to me, Margot." He gripped her shoulders.

Abruptly she stood and faced him, walking about in her garter and her brassiere, smiling, her slim hips wiggling in the full sunlight. He turned, his arms spread, his palms facing upward in helplessness.

"Look at me," he grunted. "Damn it, girl, take me." The intercom buzzed. "Don't bother me for now," he almost hissed into the machine, and turned back.

Margot stared in delight at his pulsating cock, throbbing with purple veins, begging for her attentions.

"Well, I don't know," she seemed to muse. But really, she craved that thick, enormous prod facing her. Margot sat down against one of the white couches and spread her knees, fully exposing herself. She gazed at Malcolm beginning to walk frantically about the room, trying to still his member that had taken on a life of its own. Her own cunt was moist with hunger.

"Margot," Malcolm grunted, as she slid down on the ground, gazing up at him. "Have me," he pleaded softly.

Margot lay back on both arms, staring up, her breasts like firm melons. She nodded, stretched out her arms to him and spread her legs. With a groan of contentment, he joined her on the floor—exactly as she wished it to happen.

More Erotica from Headline:

Lena's Story

❧❧❧❧❧

Anonymous

**The Adventures of
a Parisian
Queen of the Night**

Irene was once a dutiful wife. Until, forsaking the
protection of her husband, she embarked on a
career as a sensuous woman: Lena, the most
sought-after mistress in *fin de siècle* Paris. Yet
despite the luxury, the champagne and the lavish
attentions of her lovers, Lena feels her life is
incomplete. She still longs for the one love that
can satisfy her, the erotic pinnacle of a life of
unbridled pleasure . . .

More titillating erotica available from Headline

FICTION/EROTICA   0 7472 3334 9   £2.99

Sweet Fanny

The erotic education of a Regency maid

Faye Rossignol

'From the time I was sixteen until the age of thirty-two I "spread the gentlemen's relish" as the saying goes. In short, I was a Lady of Pleasure.'

Fanny, now the Comtesse de C---, looks back on a lifetime of pleasure, of experiment in the myriad Arts of Love. In letters to her granddaughter and namesake, she recounts the erotic education of a young girl at the hands of a mysterious Comte – whose philosophy of life carries hedonism to voluptuous extremes – and his partners in every kind of sin. There is little the young Fanny does not experience – and relate in exquisite detail to the recipient of her remarkably revealing memoirs.

Coming soon from Headline
SWEET FANNY'S DIARIES

FICTION/EROTICA   0 7472 3275 X   £2.99

More Erotic Fiction from Headline:

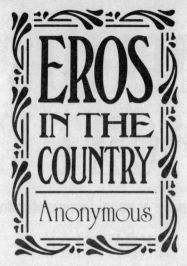

EROS IN THE COUNTRY

Anonymous

Being the saucy adventures of sweet, virginal Sophie, her lusty brother Frank and young Andrew, the village lad with a taste for pleasure – a youthful trio who engage in some not-so-innocent bedplay.

Their enthusiastic experiments come to an abrupt halt when they are discovered in flagrante and sent from home in disgrace. And so begins an erotic odyssey of sensual discovery to titillate even the most jaded imagination . . .

Her tender flesh prey to lascivious lechers of both high and low estate, Sophie seeks refuge in the arms of the students of Cambridge, ever keen to enlarge on their worldly knowledge. Meanwhile Andrew is bound by the silken lash of desire, voluptuous ladies provoking him to ever more unbearable heights of ecstasy.

EROS IN THE COUNTRY – where every excess of lust and desire is encountered, experienced and surpassed . . .

FICTION/EROTICA   0 7472 3145 1   £2.99

MAID'S NIGHT IN

A novel of smouldering eroticism

ANONYMOUS

The darkly arousing story of Beatrice, a
nubile Victorian newly-wed, lately
estranged from her husband and left to
the charge of her mysterious aunt and
uncle. Ushered into a shadowy Gothic
world of champagne and sensuality,
the young ingenue finds herself
transformed into the prime player in
exotic games of lust and power. *Maid's
Night In* is a disturbingly erotic
revelation of Victorian sexual desire.

EROS
IN THE
FAR EAST

Anonymous

Recuperating from a dampening experience at the hands of one of London's most demanding ladies, the ever-dauntless Andy resolves to titil.ate his palate with foreign pleasures: namely a return passage to Siam. After a riotously libidinous ocean crossing, he finds himself in southern Africa, sampling a warm welcome from its delightfully unabashed natives.

Meanwhile, herself escaping an unsavoury encounter in the English lakes, his lovely cousin Sophia sets sail for Panama and thence to the intriguing islands of Hawaii – and a series of bizarrely erotic tribal initiations which challenge the limits of even her sensuous imagination!

After a string of energetically abandoned frolics, Andy and Sophia fetch up in the stately city of Singapore, a city which holds all the dangerously piquant pleasures of the mysterious East, and an adventure more outrageous than any our plucky pair have yet encountered. . .

Follow Andy and Sophia's other erotic exploits:
EROS IN THE COUNTRY   EROS IN TOWN
EROS IN THE NEW WORLD   EROS ON THE GRAND TOUR

FICTION/EROTICA   0 7472 3449 3   £3.50

CREMORNE GARDENS

ANONYMOUS

**An erotic romp from the
libidinous age of the Victorians**

UPSTAIRS, DOWNSTAIRS . . . IN MY LADY'S CHAMBER

Cast into confusion by the wholesale defection of their
domestic staff, the nubile daughters of Sir Paul Arkley are
forced to throw themselves on the mercy of the handsome
young gardener Bob Goggin. And Bob, in turn, is only
too happy to throw himself on the luscious and oh-so-
grateful form of the delicious Penny.

Meanwhile, in the Mayfair mansion of Count Gewirtz of
Galicia, the former Arkley employees prepare a feast
intended to further the Count's erotic education of the
voluptuous singer Vaźelina Volpe – and destined to
degenerate into the kind of wild and secret orgy for which
the denizens of Cremorne Gardens are justly famous . . .

*Here are forbidden extracts drawn from the notorious
chronicles of the Cremorne – a society of hedonists and
debauchees, united in their common aim to glorify the
pleasures of the flesh!*

A selection of bestsellers
from Headline

FICTION

ONE GOLDEN NIGHT	Elizabeth Villars	£4.99 □
HELL HATH NO FURY	M R O'Donnell	£4.99 □
CONQUEST	Elizabeth Walker	£4.99 □
HANNAH	Christine Thomas	£4.99 □
A WOMAN TO BE LOVED	James Mitchell	£4.99 □
GRACE	Jan Butlin	£4.99 □
THE STAKE	Richard Laymon	£4.99 □
THE RED DEFECTOR	Martin L Gross	£4.99 □
LIE TO ME	David Martin	£4.99 □
THE HORN OF ROLAND	Ellis Peters	£3.99 □

NON-FICTION

LITTLE GREGORY	Charles Penwarden	£4.99 □
PACIFIC DESTINY	Robert Elegant	£5.99 □

SCIENCE FICTION AND FANTASY

HERMETECH	Storm Constantine	£4.99 □
TARRA KHASH: HROSSAK!	Brian Lumley	£3.99 □
DEATH'S GREY LAND	Mike Shupp	£4.50 □
The Destiny Makers 4		

*All Headline books are available at your local bookshop or newsagent,
or can be ordered direct from the publisher. Just tick the titles you want
and fill in the form below. Prices and availability subject to change without
notice.*

Headline Book Publishing PLC, Cash Sales Department, PO Box 11,
Falmouth, Cornwall, TR10 9EN, England.

Please enclose a cheque or postal order to the value of the cover price
and allow the following for postage and packing:
UK: 80p for the first book and 20p for each additional book ordered up
to a maximum charge of £2.00
BFPO: 80p for the first book and 20p for each additional book
OVERSEAS & EIRE: £1.50 for the first book, £1.00 for the second
book and 30p for each subsequent book.

Name ....

Address ....

....

....